MW00939284

SATAN'S SEED

An End Times Supernatural Thriller

By

Bob Mitchell

Also by Bob Mitchell

Rome, Babylon the Great and Europe

The Messiah Code

Antichrist, the Vatican and the Great Deception

The Post Tribulation Rapture of the Church

Signs of the End

You Can Predict the Future
(Gospel evangelistic booklet)

The Temple of the Antichrist

There were Giants in the Earth

God's Amazing Word

The Rapture (What Does the Scripture Say?)

Introduction

This book is a work of fiction interwoven with historical facts and present day events, along with ancient prophecies that are, at the time of writing, still future but according to many, on our near horizon...

Genesis 3:15 (God speaking to Satan)
And I will put enmity between thee and the woman, and between thy seed and her seed; it shall bruise thy head, and thou shalt bruise his heel.

PROLOGUE

THE FEAST OF THE BEAST

The young woman swept into the hotel with the ease of someone who knows what they want and how to get it. Eyes turned to watch her. Some onlookers commented she acted as if she owned the place.

She did, and she reveled in the lustful, staring eyes of the men and green-eyed envious looks of their women as she made her way across the lobby.

Raven like hair hanging past her shoulders, blending into the dark fur of the coat she had worn since leaving the autumn chill of Paris earlier that day.

An oval face framing her high cheekbones beneath dark, seductive eyes. She had it all including the full red lips and a body that had seduced many men, leaving them emotionally ruined for want of her drug-induced, fleeting sexual passions.

At just thirty-five years, the Comtesse De Mourney looked ten years younger as she approached the hotel manager, who seeing her arrive unexpectedly turned a shade of sickening gray for fear she may find something amiss.

"Madame la Comtesse," he groveled. "Such an unexpected pleasure."

"Don't lie, François. Your face shows how thrilled you are to see me."

"Oh, Madam, no..."

She waved a dismissive hand. "It's okay. I am here only for the next two or three days. Whatever is wrong, I am sure you will, as always, put right?" she lowered her head and looked up at him menacingly then relaxed with a laugh that had captivated and hypnotized so many admirers.

François Belmont was no exception. He melted at the sight of those smiling red lips he had so longed to kiss since taking up his position four years earlier after moving to the south of France as manager of the Hotel Azure in Villefranche-Sur-Mer.

"Of course, of course, Madame. Your will, your slightest desire is our command." He nervously cleared his throat.

Michelle de Mourney knew she had the power to make any man dissolve with just a smile. She had possessed it since childhood, twisting her late father and mother around her little fingers, drawing out of them everything and anything she wished for.

Her mother, an Assyrian Jewess from Turkey, had married into French aristocracy and Michelle de Mourney was especially proud of her Assyrian, Jewish ancestry. She was born in Turkey as her mother had wished it and her dual nationality served her well as she traveled throughout Europe and the Middle East on both business and pleasure.

She had inherited the hotel Azure and the title from her uncle, the Comte when he passed away at the age of eighty-nine. Being an orphan since the death of her parents in a plane disaster some years earlier and possessing a mind several years older, infinitely more evil and more devilishly conniving than, as some said, the Devil himself, she took up the reins of ownership with relish.

Today's sudden arrival was a half anticipated surprise for the hotel staff. Michelle de Mourney often came on a whim to escape the dullness of Paris when the partying season had faded and then to Ankara for the winter. But today was no whim. Others had planned this time meticulously for her. Tonight was to be her night of triumph: a triumph that would set in motion the final defeat of the cursed God and Messiah of Israel.

"My dear François. As efficient as ever."

"Have my bags taken to my private suite…it is prepared, as always?"

"As always, Madame la Comtesse, should you arrive as you have today. We are always prepared, ready and honored to receive Madam at any hour, night or day. Did Madam drive or fly."

"Oh, I came in my plane to Nice. Ferdinand, my driver, drove down earlier and met me at the airport."

"Madame, if he had brought your luggage here directly…"

"Then I would not have surprised you, would I?" Belmont bowed and pressed the bell for the porter who appeared as if by magic from a side room.

"Madame la Comtesse's luggage, Michael, at once."

Michael rushed toward the entrance where Ferdinand was unloading her cases from the Porsche 959 parked at the entrance. He hastily placed them onto a small luggage cart and wheeled them through the milieu of guests in the lobby to the private elevator where he pressed the only button available, taking him to the private penthouse suite that overlooked the bay.

One button up and one button down.

After depositing the cases, he quickly ensured the accommodation was as the Countess would expect it to be. He unlocked the balcony doors and slid them open, making sure the loungers were clean and in the perfect position to catch the afternoon sun.

For a moment, Michael stood and admired the view across the bay. The sun glinted on the gentle waves, making them sparkle like myriads of diamonds as they gently broke on the sand. Beyond them, the Mediterranean spread out as far as the eye could see in a panoramic display of opal blue while white-sailed yachts and larger cruisers gently rose and fell with the tide.

The hotel stood on the edge of the bay with only the main road to Nice separating it from the sea. The red-roofed buildings behind the Azure spread upward toward the cliffs that led to the French Alps beyond.

The boy spun around as the door of the penthouse opened behind him. The Comtesse, accompanied by Ferdinand, threw her fur to the settee and kicked off her shoes. Michael bowed and asked, "Does Madame la Comtesse require any further assistance?"

"Thank you, no, not immediately. But I would

like some water and fresh fruit sent up a little later, after I have rested. In about an hour."

"Of course, Madame la Comtesse." He bowed again and backed out as if leaving royalty.

After making sure all was correct, Ferdinand saluted and made as if to leave, but she stopped him. "Thank you, Ferdi, I will call you in a couple of days. Until then I will drive the Porsche. I have booked you into a room a couple of floors below. Take some time by the pool and relax for a change." She removed her pearls from around her neck. "And Ferdi, I do not want to be contacted over the next few days. Clear? Any messages you have for me can wait. This should be enough to keep you happy if you keep away from the tables. If you get short of funds, just let me know."

She handed him a bundle of notes and his room key.

Her unnatural generosity took him by surprise. Usually, she would have checked him into a cheaper hotel, and she never gave him more than he needed for a week's stay.

"Oh, Madame, that is too much. I certainly do not need such an amount for a few days."

"You know, Ferdi, that is why I have you with me. You are the most honest and discreet man I know. Others would simply have taken the cash and left. And many would have been calling the tabloids to reveal everything I may involve myself with down here. But you..."

"Madam, I was with your uncle, la Comte, for fifteen years before his passing. I regard it an honor to be permitted to work for you in any capacity," he bowed humbly. "And may I say, Madam Comtesse, I have no interest in the tables, I hate the tabloids and avoid the gutter press," he lied. He loved all three.

She knew it, but said nothing and smiled.

"Thank you as always. Now go, enjoy the next few days until I call you. I have some important duties to perform while here."

"Certainly, Madame la Comtesse, and thank you," he turned and exited the suite.

It was a cat and mouse game they both seemed to enjoy. He, knowing she was an evil, vile creature that fed on men's weaknesses and belonged to several odd secret societies. And she, knowing he knew all the above and fed the tabloids with the occasional piece of news about her. As long as he didn't go too far earning his extra pocket money.

It was a dangerous game they both played: one that could have a perilous end for one or both of them if they played the game badly.

As he walked toward the elevator, Ferdi

began to whistle softly. He stopped and glanced back. *"What duties does she have down here? All her interests are in Turkey, Israel, and Paris. She has always treated me with respect, but all this cash for a few days? What is she up to? Why does she so want me out of her hair for the next few days? A new lover? A new business venture? No, probably another poor idiot sucked in by her charms. But whatever, it could mean extra cash for me if I keep my wits about me and watch what she does."*

He pulled the money from his trouser pocket.

"And in the end, do I care? Not a bit." He whistled again and swiftly vanished into the elevator in case she changed her mind and came after him to retrieve some of the notes.

Later that evening Ferdi was sitting alone at the hotel bar. He began eyeing a stunning blonde at a table a few feet away from him. She noticed him staring.

"Blast it. I'm not used to this," he cursed and turned away.

"Excuse me," she spoke in a stage whisper. He didn't turn. "Monsieur, you at the bar." He felt the embarrassment rising. She was going to accuse him of ogling her. She, a slim, thirty-something dressed to kill in a red mini-dress that showed every contour of her body as if she had been poured into it and he, sixty-two and balding, wearing Levis, a white open-necked shirt, and deck shoes. "I am sorry, Mademoiselle, do you mean me?" "*Of course she did, you idiot.*"

She laughed, "Unless you have an invisible friend beside you."

He gave in, "*Get it over with quick. Let her give me an earful and accuse me of being a dirty lecher. Apologize, don't cause a scene.*" Taking a deep breath, he turned and faced her.

"Before you scold me for looking at you, I apologize. You caught my eye as the most beautiful woman to cross my path in what has been a very long, tiresome day. Again, my apologies," he bowed politely.

"Well, that's the best backhanded come on I've heard in a while," she laughed again. A soft, gentle laugh that to Ferdie seemed for some reason to be full of promise.

"You are staying at the hotel?" He attempted to sound what he was...old enough to be her father.

"On my way to my sister's wedding in Venice in two days. I leave in the morning, but I've had few days here to kill before then so..."

"So, a chance to chill, I believe the expression is nowadays?"

"Indeed. And you?"

"Chilling."

"A man of mystery. I like men of mystery."
She made her way to the bar and hoisted herself onto a stool beside him.

"Carol Manning," they shook hands.

"Ferdinand," he replied.

"Ferdinand...?"

"Just Ferdinand or Ferdi," he smiled.

She stuck her tongue between her perfect teeth and narrowed her eyes. "Very mysterious. I like you even more."

"May I buy you a drink, Carol?"
She rolled her eyes and smiled. "Drinks at the bar are so expensive, don't you think?"

"Do we have a choice?"

"I have two bottles of wine in my room crying out for someone to open them."

"*I can't believe I am about to do this,*" Ferdi felt his blood rising. "So...?"

"So, I am alone, you appear to be alone, and now we are together. Why don't we go to my room and put my wine bottles out of their misery?"

His eyes ran over her face and body. She was perfection on legs inviting him to her room.

Suddenly, out of the corner of his eyes, he saw the Comtesse enter the lobby and make for the exit to the car park. She was dressed in black from head to toe. A full-length cape and hood, jogger bottoms and jet black loafers.

"Where is she off to at..." he glanced at his wristwatch "almost eleven?"

Carol Manning's eyes widened. "Looking at your watch, Ferdinand? Am I that boring?"

He apologized and then had an impulsive thought.

"Carol, do you have a car?"

"Yes, but I thought..."

"How would you like to have an adventure this evening?"

"I had the feeling I was about to have one," she replied with a pout.

He ignored her pleading look. "Where are you parked? Come on; this will be fun. There's someone I want to follow. Are you game?"

"You mean like a detective?"She threw her head back and laughed.

"Like Bond, come on," he grabbed her hand, and the two swiftly went to the door about thirty seconds behind the Comtesse.

"Be as quiet as you can," he put his finger to his lips. "The person we are following is right ahead of us."

"The woman in the black outfit? Your girlfriend?"

"No. Someone I work for. Tonight she is going to some private assignation, I am sure, and I want to see where."

"Why? I'm not so sure about this. I don't want to get into any trouble," she began to slow down and pull away from his grip on her hand.

"No, Carol. This is a bit of fun, snooping. No fear of any trouble. If there is, it will be me, not you who gets it in the neck."

"Sure?"

"Certain. I wouldn't want you in any bother. You're okay. Believe me. I want to get something on my boss, for a change. She seems to know all about me and my private life, even though she thinks I don't know how much she knows. So I want to turn the tables and perhaps if I am lucky tonight, get a bit of juicy scandal. Something I can hold onto…a kind of backup plan if ever she decides to get rid of me for any reason. I have a good job, and I don't want to lose it. But we are all getting older, and I need a get out of jail card.

"Tonight she is acting completely out of character, and I think she's off to see someone or do something she doesn't want anyone to know about. I am certain of it. She has been mixing with some peculiar people over the last few years. Shady, powerful and very secretive people. I can't say why, but tonight I think she may be meeting up with some of them. I just want to see what she is up to. Put it down to sheer male intuition. We'll see where she goes; then we'll come back and visit your wine cellar and have a debate on the world situation," he winked. Deal?"

"Well, okay. Never let it be said Carol Manning isn't up for some fun," she bit her lip, thought for a moment and then grinned. "Let's go for it."

They waited until they saw the Comtesse get into the Porsche and drive toward the exit leading onto the street. They raced to Carol's car, a little red coupe. Ferdi barely managed to squeeze his six feet five inches into it as Carol slid easily into the driver's seat and set off, heading north toward the outskirts of town.

"Keep well back from her. I don't want her to see she's being followed."

"No problem, Mister Bond," she laughed excitedly as the warm evening breeze raced through the open car turning her blonde hair into a trail of light behind her.

They kept well behind de Mourney, almost losing her once or twice, but although the road leading into the hills behind the city was full of hairpin bends, it had very few turnoffs and after losing her for a few moments, she would come back into view.

After following for almost thirty minutes, they saw the Porsche turn down a dusty side road leading into a heavily wooded area. Carol was about to follow when she noticed the Comtesse had pulled to a halt just beyond the first line of trees and parked alongside several other cars.

They drove on for a few yards, then pulled into a lay-by at the side of the road to avoid any oncoming traffic.

"What on earth is she doing out here? There are no houses or hotels...nothing," Fredi whispered as if de Mourney could hear him speak from a hundred yards away.

She exited the Porsche and headed deeper into the forest wrapped in the cape with the hood pulled up over her head.

"Let's go back now," Carol pleaded. "This is getting weird, and I don't like it. Why would she park up here and go alone into the woods at this time of night? It's eleven thirty, for goodness sake."

"That's just what I intend to find out," said Ferdinand. "I think this is going to be my insurance premium if ever she decides to be rid of me for any reason. If she does decide to kick me out of this job, I'll hopefully lay this on her table and walk away with a well-earned payoff and a bonus. I've been waiting for years to catch her out, and now I think my time has come. I am sure whatever it is she is planning to do in the woods at this time of night has to be something huge. Something she wouldn't want to read in the tabloids."

He gripped Carol's hand. "Come on. We'll spend just ten minutes here, and then I promise we'll go back to the Hotel." The girl heaved a sigh and shook her head.

"I'm not so sure there's no danger in this."

"Danger?" he laughed. "The only danger is to her purse strings if I catch her in some secret rendezvous she obviously doesn't want anyone to know about. All her previous affairs were out in the open, and she didn't give a hoot who knew. But this...this is different. In all the years I have known her I have never known her to act so secretively. She has been to a few screwball secret meetings with the European elite. But she has never done anything quite like this. Are you game? I'll pay you for your trouble?"

"What? Are you crazy?"

"And you can sit tight here and wait for me. If I am not back in fifteen minutes you can turn the car around and leave me. I'll find my own way back. Look, she's heading into the woods, and I'll lose her if I don't move now. Cash for fifteen minutes snooping or shall we drive back for a drink and say goodnight?" He held a pile of notes in his hand.

Carol took one look and lifted them. "Well, I am out of here in the morning, so an hour's drive out here and back plus fifteen minutes work snooping on your boss in the woods," she licked her lips. "There's almost six hundred dollars here. This, for seventy five minutes work? My friend, you have a deal. But fifteen minutes and fifteen only. Not a second over or I'm gone, and you'll be walking home."

"Then let's snoop," Ferdi smiled as she pocketed the notes and he climbed out of the car.

"No, you snoop, I'll wait here."

Creeping through the woods in the middle of the night with no light to guide or warn of any obstacles is never an easy task. Ferdi tried to be as cat-like as possible, but he felt as if every broken twig sounded like a gunshot. Several times overhanging branches and unseen divots took him by surprise scraping his arms and almost twisting his ankles.

At last, he heard voices and could see lights a little ahead of him in a clearing. He began to wonder if this had been such a good idea after all. He'd convinced the girl to come with him on a crazy adventure, and now he was scratched, tired and about to see his boss meet someone she obviously didn't want anyone to know about. Was it all worth the effort? He could have been in bed with this beauty. Instead, he was scratched, dirty, laying on the ground in the middle of the night behind a bush in a forest.

Suddenly his ears pricked up.

"Is that chanting I hear?"

He strained his ears in the darkness as a breeze swept through the trees, bringing with it the unmistakable sound of voices and a waft of incense. It wasn't singing, but a low, guttural, mumbling, rhythmic chant.

He inched his way forward through the undergrowth until, lying on his stomach, he parted the branches of a small bush that concealed him.

As his eyes became accustomed to the night, he could make out a clearing.

Several lighted black candelabrum were arranged in a large circle. In the center of the circle was an oblong stone about four feet high and around seven feet in length laying horizontally like a huge altar stone.

He expected to see the Comtesse, but she had vanished. What he did see, gathered on the opposite side of the stone, turned his blood cold. A group of more than twenty masked men and women in black robes in a line, each carrying an upturned human skull.

One of the men stepped forward and raised the skull he held toward the altar. The others did the same but stayed behind him.

As he raised the skull he cried, "Oh, Lord Satan, we, your devoted and unworthy servants, come this night to honor you on this hallowed evening of this great Feast of the Beast. It is an exceptional night, oh Lord, and we entreat you to come and honor us with your presence as we offer ourselves afresh to your service.

"Tonight we call upon you to fulfill the words and the promise of the ancients. We have waited so many years to see the great work come to reality. Oh, great one, we beg of you, come, come, Satan and bring forth from your very being the sacred seed of the serpent. Let the seed come."

The foul group joined him, chanting in

unison "Let him come, let the seed rise."

The apparent leader held his hand aloft.

"Bring the sacrifice." A small goat that had been tethered out of sight was brought forward by one of the group and held down on the altar. The leader held a long, ornately decorated curved dagger in his free hand. With one swift blow he slit the throat of the helpless, struggling animal and with a cry of devilish delight, he collected the dying animal's lifeblood as it pumped into the skull.

The devotees behind the altar had now become a baying mob, desperate to share in the vile act. They rushed forward to catch the dripping blood into the skulls they held and then began a slow dance around the altar, as from some well-concealed position discordant music began to play slow, rhythmic drumming, accompanied by the sound of a flute.

As the music became more discordant and wild, they began to throw themselves into a frenzy, drinking the blood and crying, "Hail, Satan. Hail, Lucifer. Hail, the promised one who is to come: the seed of the serpent."

Ferdinand felt sick in his stomach. The nausea was almost overwhelming. He turned to move away in utter disgust. As he did the leader of the group, let out a scream.

"He is here. He is here! Look, my children, he is here." The man was pointing to a mound at the side of the altar. A green swirling mist had appeared and slowly within it, Ferdi's bulging eyes could make out the form of a giant goat-like creature standing on its hind legs. Goat-like, yet in some strange way human. The head was that of a huge goat with large horns. The torso and arms were human. Below the waist, all was fur with the hind legs of a goat.

Ferdi tried to tear his eyes away from the horrific scene, but he was almost mesmerized, wanting to leave and yet needing to witness this unbelievable ceremony.

The creature spoke. The voice seemed old yet strong. The words it uttered were so utterly evil, more than any Ferdinand had ever heard and though not a religious man it repulsed him to the heart making him want to vomit.

"I, Lucifer, have come. Tonight I answer the call of the ages to produce a seed in answer to the accursed offspring of the Hebrew God. At the cross, he thought he had defeated me. But we have waited until this time, this moment, to give him our answer. You shall not win, Yeshua. I, Satan will be Lord of this earth and through my chosen one, my seed, I will utterly destroy any hope of your return to rule this planet. It is mine, and all your pathetic creation will ultimately bow and worship me alone through my chosen seed." He shook his fist toward the heavens as the bellowing mob went into raptures, screaming and throwing themselves into all kinds of contortions before this physical appearance of evil.

"Bring me the chosen vessel." The creature commanded.

Up until that moment Ferdinand had forgotten about his mistress, but suddenly de Mourney appeared from the darkness of the woods. Now dressed in a golden cloak and shepherded by two hooded men, one on either side, she walked majestically toward the beast and the altar. The surrounding candles lit the entire scene with an odd glow as the breeze swirled through the trees above them.

The Countess stopped short of the beast and bowed in submission.

"I am here, oh great one. As the stupid Jewess, Miriam, gave herself to birth the one who is called the Christ, Messiah, the seed of the woman Eve, so I now offer myself in humble adoration to bear your seed, oh, Lord of darkness, to birth the seed of the serpent, the beast. I desire to carry the one the followers of the Jewish Messiah call the Antichrist.

"May I be worthy, oh mighty Lucifer, the bringer of true light and wisdom, to bear your seed and may he destroy once and for all time the seed of the woman and his followers. May the supposed prophecies of our defeat never be realized and may your seed rise from within my womb to rule the world and defeat the cursed Jewish God-man on his return. Grant this, oh Lucifer. I offer myself to you now."

She threw the cloak to the ground, revealing her total nakedness as she climbed onto the altar and laid her perfectly sculptured body down in submission.

The creature from hell raised its voice in a howl of victory. It leaped from the hillock onto the altar and lowered itself upon the supine, body of the Countess de Morney as she visibly quivered with excitement and devilish lust.

The worshipping onlookers suddenly raised their voices in praise as they, too, threw their robes to the ground and cavorted and danced naked around the altar where the grotesque sexual act was being consummated.

Ferdinand could no longer stand the sight of this unbelievable horror and closed his eyes as once again his stomach heaved involuntarily.

Taking one last look, to lock the sight into his memory, he began to turn and move away from the odious scene. But as he did so, the abominable creature atop of the Countess spun its head and looked directly into Ferdinand's terrified eyes; its hand reached out pointing toward him.

"Vile intruder! Take him." It spat the words like venom. For a moment the participants in the ceremony were taken by surprise. They ceased their wild celebrating and turned in Ferdinand's direction.

Thankfully, they could not see him hiding in the darkness of the undergrowth. But the foul beast continuing to impregnate the Countess knew he was there.

"There," it howled. "There is an intruder in the camp of Lucifer." They made a move toward Ferdinand's hiding place.

For a moment he was frozen in stark, cold terror at being discovered. Then, he came to his senses and took off through the trees, running for his very life. Fortunately for him, the guests were not keen to follow their master's orders and give chase naked into the woods. As they quickly began to gather their cloaks from the ground, this gave Ferdinand a few moments lead as he raced back toward the road and the safety of the car he hoped and prayed was still waiting for him.

He sprinted, not caring what branches or potholes may be in his way. Completely terrified out of his wits he sped toward the highway, the bushes clawing at him, scratching his face and drawing blood as if they had sprung to life, reaching out trying to prevent his escape. He fell headlong into the dirt, but quickly picked himself up and headed directly for the road.

He left the woods where, to his utter relief, Carol was still waiting, having already turned the car around so that it was facing the direction from which they had originally come.

"My Lord, you are as white as a sheet, and you're bleeding." She gasped as he jumped in beside her.

"Just drive. For heaven's sake, just drive. Get us out of here now! I'm being chased."

Hearing the sound of the demonically driven pursuers coming from the darkness of the woods, Carol pushed her foot to the floor and the car shot off in the direction of the distant city lights while all around was complete darkness.

"What happened? Tell me, Ferdi."

"Best you don't know. You wouldn't believe me if I told you." He ran a trembling hand over his ashen face as the sweat ran down the back of his neck. "Just get us back to town, and I suggest you grab your things and leave with me right away."

"What do you mean? Where are we going?"

"Anywhere, anywhere you like, just get us away from here now, tonight."

They drove in silence. Ferdi was trembling and gazing ahead into the darkness as if in a trance. Every few moments he spun around to see if anyone was following. But all was quiet.

After a while, he spoke softly through trembling lips. "We must get far away from them."

"*Them*?" Carol frowned. "You mean your boss and her lover or whoever she met out there?"

"Her lover," Ferdi began to laugh, almost hysterically. "Her lover. If you can call some living, breathing demonic creature her lover, then yes."

"Ferdi you are beginning to scare me. What are you talking about?"

"I mean, as far as I can understand it, my boss has just had sex with the Devil himself and is planning on having his baby, the Antichrist." Carol looked at him in disbelief and began to laugh. "Ferdi, stop it." She pulled the car to the side of the road. "What is going on? Stop fooling. Who did your boss visit in the woods?"

"Satan, Lucifer, whoever you call him. My God, she allowed that thing to have sex with her. What foul, diseased brain would allow such a thing?" He buried his face in his hands and involuntarily shuddered.

"Carol, just drive. Please, just get us back to town."

She looked at him for a moment as she realized he was serious. Taking a deep breath, she decided to do as he asked and wait until he had calmed down before asking any more.

As they began the steep, winding drive down toward the lights of the city, she started pumping the brake pedal.

"The brakes. The brakes have gone." She was ramming her foot to the floor, but nothing was happening.

"Pull over and switch off the ignition."

"I...I can't. The steering is locked," she screamed in terror.

The car quickly gained momentum as it sped down the hill. Carol frantically pumped the brakes and tried to pull the steering wheel toward the side of the road. But it was no use: the car was out of her control.

Ferdi shouted, "We'll have to jump for it."

But as they moved to a standing position, the car lurched, throwing them back into the seats.

It was then they saw the cliff coming toward them at breakneck speed. There was no escape. They both screamed as the car smashed through the barrier at the side of the road, catapulting them high into the air a hundred feet above the Mediterranean shore below.

Ferdi threw himself across her body in a vain attempt to protect her from the fall.

In a moment it was all over. The car plunged head-on into the rocks with a dull, sickening crump, falling sideways into the water. Their two bodies lay entangled in the wreckage as the incoming tide lapped around them.

The next day, the local papers reported a tragic accident on a dangerous part of the road into Villefranche-Sur-Mer. The driver had apparently lost control as no mechanical fault was discovered. As a result of the car's one hundred foot plunge, the driver had died at once alongside her male passenger.

It took three months for the bodies to be released due to the local police investigation, autopsy reports and inquest results.

The verdict: accidental death due to dangerous driving. Once the bodies were released, the Comtesse de Mourney attended the joint funerals of both the deceased.

After placing a spray of orchids on both

coffins and paying her respects to the families and friends of the two victims, she was escorted back to her car by her new assistant.

As she left, one or two onlookers noticed the Countess wore a slight smile and even appeared to be gaining a little weight.

Just six months later she gave birth to a healthy baby boy while visiting Turkey: father, unknown.

Chapter 1
LONDON, UK.

Jack Bridger cast a bored eye around the room then, glanced at his watch, "Have I been here only two hours? Seems like four."

He remonstrated with himself. This was a plum job. One he had dreamed of ever since entering the world of news media and crazy deadlines which have to be met or else.

Just twelve months earlier, he had been handed an offer he just couldn't refuse. His own independent news program, presenting virtually anything and interviewing anyone he wished on satellite TV. So long as OFCOM, the UK's media watchdog didn't get in his way.

After fifteen years as anchorman for a fringe network News Service in the States, he had made what he hoped was a wise career move. He moved to England with his wife Marsha and so far it had proved to be every news man's dream. He loved London. He loved the hustle and bustle of life behind the scenes. He ate, drank and slept the planning, the setting out of news items in the order of importance; having to change them as something else hit the wire. Getting scripts ready, reading, editing and re-

reading them. Inviting guests to the program only to sometimes have them cancel at the last minute, leaving him to wing it, ad-libbing and juggling the script without the audience knowing anything had gone awry. It was a high wire act he loved performing before the growing audience tuning in to the new station.

The Independent News Station:"I.N.S." to those who worked there, was rapidly becoming a regular service people could trust to give the real news and not a doctored, sanitized version of events. The founders, Hal and Stacey Montgomery, had sunk a huge chunk of their fortune into birthing the station in the USA and had now embarked on a new station based in the middle of London.

Over the years they had grown frustrated and angry at the spin doctoring of news events that had every hope of being explosive, but had wound up being a damp squib thanks to the chicken-hearted heads of news corporations who had to cow-tow to both the visible government and the shadow government: the secret power behind the power, run by the global elite.

Hal knew from friends in the media industry that what appeared on the nightly news was often never the real story. He even had one friend "*commit suicide*" though Hal knew full well he had died as a result of knowing too much about a particular politician's love life. He was on the verge of offering the story to a major international magazine but was found dead with a single gunshot wound to the head and a pistol nestling conveniently beside the corpse.

Real life behind the news was very often a whole different story. It was a horrible world. One Hal and the team loved to expose to anyone who had the guts to open their eyes and see what went on behind much of the façade that passed daily for world events.

Often, the viewers having their evening meal at home received the heavily doctored version of the day's events: rarely the "down in the mud" naked truth.

Now Hal and Stacey were out to bring the real news behind the news. They didn't give two hoots what people said as long as what "I.N.S." presented was accurate and could be substantiated.

Not to suggest the newborn babe had no enemies who tried to kill it off at birth. But, thank God, so far they had beaten off all opposition with a team of exceptional lawyers and script editors who knew just how far to push the envelope. Now, with Jack Bridger on board bringing many of his devoted fans with him they believed it was a match made in journalistic heaven.

Hal and Stacey loved Jack and his wife, and they loved them in return. Not many employees could say that of their bosses. But Jack found himself confiding in and looking for guidance from, this elderly pair of Americans. A most unlikely couple of TV bosses one could not hope to find.

Hal, a typical Texan six feet tall, broad-shouldered and hair bleached by the Texan sun, had been an oil man from his youth having joined his grandfather's Texas firm in 1963. Starting out doing anything that needed tidying or carrying; anything the more experienced hands were too busy to tend to.

He gradually moved up the ladder of experience.

Drafted into the military at the age of twenty-five, he served as a medic during the Vietnam war. Following his discharge in 1975, he married Stacey, the bubbly blue-eyed little Texan redhead with whom he had been pen friending while overseas.

As he set foot back on American soil for the first time in two years, she was waiting for their first face to face date. It was love from the moment they saw each other in the flesh, and they married within weeks of his homecoming.

Hal then launched his own rigging business with his grandfather's help, making his first million dollars within the next few years.

By the time he was pushing sixty he had made over two hundred million and felt it was time for a new adventure.

He and Stacey set up I.N.S., and after some years as the viewing figures soared they sold the home, they had shared since their wedding and headed for Europe, settling in London taking the whole business along with them.

After months of meetings with journalists, politicians, bankers, and lawyers, The Independent News Service was born. A handful of excited journalists, technicians, directors, and producers *"wet the baby's head"* in the Queen Anne room of the Westminster Arms, a stone's throw from the Houses of Parliament. In this watering hole of politicians, journalists, civil servants, and actors the *great adventure*, as Hal called it, was launched. Just one year later Hal headhunted Jack Bridger and Jack, who was as frustrated as Hal being surrounded by an army of PC peddlers, was only too happy to leave for some fresh air and a more daring approach to life.

What Bridger couldn't bear was the fact that this meeting in Hal's executive office, impressive as it was, was now moving into the world of financial reports and graphs showing successful sales of station advertising time to different companies.

This was not Jack's area at all. He had attended the meeting to discuss guests for the next two months and barring any major world events when he would have to squeeze someone in to give their expert opinion; he had concluded his part in the evening.

He clenched his square jaw suppressing a yawn. His thoughts drifted, wondering if Hal's club just off Trafalgar Square in Whitehall would still be open. All he had eaten since breakfast was a burger and coffee at lunchtime. It was already 9:30 p.m. and at this rate by the time he arrived home in Dartford, his wife Marsha would be in bed and not exactly in the mood to cook him a dinner.

"She'll know I'm going to be late. All the same, I should call her," Jack thought to himself.

There was a pause in the conversation and Jack took his chance.

"Sorry Hal, but do you still need me?"

Hal gently rolled his marker pen between his thumb and forefinger.

"Actually, Jack, I do need to talk to you in a few minutes in private. Why? Is there someplace you need to be?"

"Other than bed," he laughed. "Not at all. But I should call Marsha and let her know I'll be later than usual."

"By all means: we'll be finished here in a moment. Make the call in the outer office and tell her we'll grab a bite in town if that's okay."

Jack excused himself and lifted his frame out of one of the leather executive chairs that surrounded the massive oak conference table around which they were seated. The eight other people, lawyers, producers, directors and Lauren, Hal's private secretary, glanced at Jack and then carried on with the next item on the agenda.

Entering Lauren's office, where she shielded Hal from all but necessary callers, Bridger opened his cell phone and sliding open the glass door stepped onto the balcony overlooking the Thames.

It was a beautiful night in London. The traffic across London Bridge was quiet for a change.

The lights were on in the Houses of

Parliament as late-night debates were always on the agenda. He breathed in the fresh air, away from the stuffy atmosphere of Hal's boardroom and dialed home. A sleep filled voice answered.

"Hello?"

"Hi, darling, 'don't think I'll be home 'til after midnight the way things are going here."

"I thought it was just a meeting to finalize guests?"

"It was that as well, but Hal is now into finances, and you know how much I love that side of things."

She laughed "As if. You have problems with our own budget, let alone the financial dealings of "I.N.S.," my sweet. So, when will you get back?"

"I was hoping to get away now, but Hal says he wants to have a private chin wag when everyone else is gone. Why I haven't the foggiest."

"Shall I prepare something and leave it out for you? I know you probably haven't eaten at all, have you?"

"You got me. Nothing but a cold burger and thick coffee. But I am guessing we'll go to his club and talk over a meal there, so don't do anything. Just get to bed. I'll be there soon."

"Okay. Drive carefully. I love you."

"Me too. See you soon."

Stepping back into Lauren's den he closed and locked the sliding door and re-entered the conference room, closing the ornate oak door behind him.

Back in their suburban home, Marsha Bridger replaced the phone. She didn't feel like going back to bed just yet so she poured herself a glass of mineral water and flopped onto the settee.

She loved Jack and the twenty years they had been married seemed to have sped by.

Having met at a Stanford University student debate, they fell in love almost immediately. She was smitten by his friendly, easy-going style. Nothing seemed to faze him at all. His tall, muscular frame and rugged face topped by a mop of thick black hair seemed to tower over her diminutive five feet three inches.

An open, fresh face framed by short shoulder length blond hair, Marsha possessed a small turned up nose and an impish little grin that swept Bridger off his feet the moment she smiled at him.

It was a whirlwind romance, and even though friends and family had warned them both against rushing into marriage after only knowing each other a few months, they had gone ahead and married as soon as they were able to get the finances together.

Although they did have their ups and downs like any average couple, the ups were far more frequent than any downs. They often said marrying was the best decision they had ever made. Now both in their early forties, they had embarked on a new adventure with Hal at the helm, and the future looked very rosy.

She sipped the water, and as she did from nowhere a sudden feeling of unease came on her. "*Why did Hal want to speak to Jack in private now? Why couldn't it wait until morning? What was so important at this time of night?*"

Chapter 2

Hal guided Bridger through the doors of the Excalibur Club and was immediately greeted by the major-domo.

"Mister Montgomery and Mister Bridger, welcome. So nice to see both of you again; your usual table, Mister Montgomery?"

"Thank you, Luigi," Hal smiled as Luigi bowed and led them to a secluded corner booth in the club restaurant.

"He's a good man, old Luigi, but a bit of a crawler," Hal said, as Luigi back-peddled to his pouncing position by the door, straightening his tie and jacket and preparing to go over his well-rehearsed lines again as another member entered.

"How do you mean?"

"Oh, he is a nice enough guy, but he uses the same line with everyone: even with the people he dislikes."

"I guess it goes with the job description," smiled Bridger.

"A wine, sir?" asked a waiter who seemed to pop up from the ground.

"Yes, we'll have the red Marqués de Murrieta Reserva."

Hal unbuttoned his jacket. "Poor Luigi. I'm

getting harsh in my old age," "In this kind of line you have to suck up to every potential customer."

"Not a lot different to us?"

"Oh no, Jack. Not us. We are never going to lower our guard and suck up to people just to get what we want."

"Never?"

"Well…maybe sometimes," Hal conceded.

"But not on a regular basis like this."

They both laughed out loud as the waiter came over and after pouring a small taster filled each man's glass.

"Okay, so...?" Bridger ran his finger around the rim of his wine glass.

"So, why have I kept you out late, away from your beautiful young wife and a nice snug bed?"

"Uh huh. I know we'll get around to it sooner or later, but I am guessing that you have something to throw my way that can't wait until the morning office conference?"

"That's one of the reasons I like you, son," Hal spoke softly, looking down at the table, folding and unfolding his napkin. "You never hold back, but are always on your toes."

"And I miss my beautiful young wife and my snug bed," Jack grinned.

"Okay, let's get to it. You are right this isn't something I want to bring up at the regular meeting tomorrow. I need to get a yes or no from you now without any pressure from people sitting around a table throwing their opinions into the ring. I trust your instinct, Jack, and your decision stays here if you decide not to take on board what I am proposing,"
Hal spoke in a half whisper.

"And if I say yes?" Bridger leaned forward to catch Hal's every word.

"Then, if it pans out, as I am hopeful it will, Jack Bridger will be a name on everyone's lips from London to all points on the compass."

"Will they be adding a few curse words to my name?"
Hal laughed. "Some, maybe: those who would have wished to beat you to the biggest exposure of the century."

"The what...?"

"You did hear me right, and I meant every word. Jack, I am in touch with someone who has a lead to a major global event."

"What major event, Hal? We are covering the escalation of events in the Middle East at the moment, and that escalation could drag the whole planet into a world war. What could be greater than a possible Third World War?"

"As President Bush Senior once said: *Read my lips*: the planned destruction of the State of Israel and a complete takeover of the Middle East including the oil fields in Israel and especially Saudi Arabia. Add to that mix the plan to bring in a global government once the dust of war settles and I think we can say such a scoop would be mega for us.

"We know the Russian, Iranian and Turkish military are operating in Syria under the guise of attempting to end the civil war. Iran is the enemy of Saudi Arabia and Israel. Turkey is anti-Israel. Russia is not a friend of Israel either and favors the Palestinians in any peace negotiations regarding the final status and a possible two-State solution to their decades-old enmity.

"Now, against all expectations, Saudi Arabia has recently become Israel's most significant Middle Eastern ally. This has only raised the stakes. Russia needs oil as does Iran, whose oil supply is rapidly dwindling.

"The Iranian economy is smarting under UN sanctions over their nuclear program. Fuel to the ant-Israel, anti-American fire was stoked even further when the USA declared Jerusalem to be Israel's capital city. Virtually the entire planet turned against Israel and the United

States as perhaps never before. My contact has, in his possession, evidence of a plan prepared by a collection of political, religious and financial masterminds, working behind the scenes with the Vatican, to allow this war to take place and Israel's destruction to be complete and total, wiping any trace of the Jewish State from the map.

"They can see the clouds forming and are rubbing their hands together with joy. It's what they want to happen so they can set in motion their plans for us all. They are using fake news, propaganda, outright lies and threats to make it happen.

"They know war means money for the stock markets and the military industrialists and they intend to get wealthier than ever on the deaths of perhaps millions. They are vile, evil people with only one goal: to make money.

"Following the war, they plan to establish some worldwide socialist government under the pretense of preventing any future war to occur for fear of global nuclear suicide."

"Hal, how can you be sure of this contact you have?"

"The man is putting his life on the line. The item he wants to hand us not only has the plans for such a war and its outcome but the names of most major players involved in this wicked scheme. From what he has told me, they are extremely powerful people. The guy knows he is as good as dead. But before he gets his wooden suit, he wants to pass what he knows on to us."

Jack shook his head. "This is incredible, Hal. Are you sure of it?"

"As sure as I can be. He reckons he has names, dates, including taped conversations and what he says is an additional planned major event due to take place after the war. All this is secured on a flash drive he somehow managed to get his hands on. I wanted to offer this to you in private. Only you, Marsha, Stacey, and I will know anything about this until we have gone over the contents of the flash drive and established its authenticity as best we can."

"Supposing I said *no way, it's a fool's errand*: if this is true, these guys are way to big for us to take on?"

"But you haven't, have you?" Hal smiled.

"Darn it, Hal, you knew I couldn't resist." Bridger fell back into the cushioned seat and laughed.

Hal's face grew serious "There is a possible downside to this, Jack."

"Apart from World War Three? In what way?"

"Don't laugh too soon, but let me ask you this," Hal pursed his lips. "Do you believe in the supernatural?"

"You're kidding me, right? Of course, I don't, Hal. Old wives tales, God, devils, goblins, ghosts, and things that go bump in the night: Santa? I left that nonsense behind when I pretended to be asleep one Christmas Eve and spotted my old man creeping into my room with a sack full of gifts. No," Bridger sat back and sipped his wine. "Left that stuff a long, long way back."

"Not even God?"

"Look, Hal, I don't want to hurt your feelings. You know how I feel about you and Stacey and I have noticed you guys never swear or cuss and are always very respectful to everyone, even the gremlins we meet in this business. I have the deepest respect for you both. So, I have always known from the start you brought a kind of Christian element along with you both. If you remember, you've given me *the gospel*, several times, but I felt it was not for me, not my line of territory."

"Okay," Hal smiled. "Of course, we are Christians. We believe in God, and both became Christians about twenty years ago."

Bridger held out his hands "Hal, that's great

for you. I love you both, but personally, I have no interest in spirituality: none at all. Can we just not go there? It freaks me out when people talk about this stuff. It's uncharted waters for Marsha and me too."

"I understand, Jack, I really do. But the reason I brought up the spiritual element was that I also have the deepest respect and love for you and Marsha. Though you may not believe in the supernatural, I have experience in that field. When I was a youngster back in the States a few of us would mess with the Ouija board. This led me to investigate the subject of the supernatural more deeply, and before long I was involved with a group that held séances and believe me, we experienced some pretty frightening goings-on. They wanted to go further, you know, late night meetings summoning spirits from the other world. I attended a few, but things that manifested in front of us, and I mean real physical beings right in front of my eyes, convinced me I should find another hobby, to put it very mildly. That's what led me to seek another way, and I discovered Jesus Christ really is alive. He changed my life and…"

"Hal…" Jack smiled. "And I thought you were a hard-nosed oil man."

Hal gave a wry grin. "Okay, okay. During a hard few months in the business, I came into contact with a group who were into the supernatural. It seemed to be an interesting diversion from the day to day business I was involved in. It turned out it was the most terrifying time of my life. Thank God Stacey wasn't in any way interested. But she let me run with it, not knowing just how deep that rabbit hole went." He seemed to gaze into space for a moment, as if remembering those times then continued.

"But now you know where I am coming from, and that's what I need to warn you about even though you may not believe what I say. It is my responsibility as your boss, and especially your friend, to place my concerns before you.

"The task I am asking you to undertake is not without danger of a very real and concrete nature: danger from physical enemies who do not want the information to surface for political, financial, military as well as certain religious and dark spiritual reasons. But danger also, from the dark side of the spirit realm, because the human elements involved have an evil purpose in stopping you ever getting close to revealing their agenda. I know from past experience and from what my contact told me these folks are involved in some very dark goings on, and I want us to expose them." He paused and looked Jack full in the face.

"Unless they kill us first."

"Well," Jack Bridger toyed with his now empty glass as he listened carefully to his boss's warnings. "I am pretty amazed you were ever involved in that spooky side of life. For me, it has never been something I would ever go near. I just cannot believe in spooks and demons. I understand you think what you experienced as a young man was real, but there are other explanations such as mass hallucination. You believe you saw something because you wanted to.

"As for the demonic and death-defying offer you have now plopped in my lap," He thoughtfully pinched his lower lip and then grinned. "I'll take it, hell or high water."

Hal began to say something, but Bridger cut him short.

"Before we go on, Hal, let me also say this: I know you believe what you say is true and I respect you for it, and I will be careful, but to be honest, I find it impossible to believe in the supernatural side of this until I experience it with my own eyes.

"The physical I can handle: been there before

in this game. The spooks, with all respect, I'll leave to you. You can pray to your God to kit me out with a suit of armor."

"That, I will most certainly do, my friend. Just remember my words, please. In taking on this venture, you are placing yourself in danger that is very real and dark: danger from a realm that is incredibly evil, intelligent and bent on preventing you and those with you from succeeding in this quest.

"I believe that apart from the military, political, global and economic repercussions this would cause, there is an ancient prophetic scenario that is taking shape right now as we speak that will have a profound and lasting effect on every human being on the planet. It is huge. I cannot overly stress, those involved will take all measures necessary to stop us. Do you understand: all measures necessary?"

Jack nodded. "I really appreciate your concern for me, Hal. It means a lot to Marsha and me. I promise I'll watch out for Old Nick if he tries to muscle in on our plans."

Realizing he was not really convincing his friend of the other-worldly danger, Hal switched the subject. "You can contact me directly on my private line. I'll tell everyone else you've decided to take the next few weeks researching a new project. That will not be a lie either; we'll look it over together.

"We have a few pre-records to fill in while you and I are researching what he hands over, so no one will be any wiser and your show will still go on air. We can cover at least three months with recordings we have to hand."

"Agreed," Smiled Bridger.

"Okay," Hal sighed, knowing deep down his warning about the supernatural would be something Jack would possibly have to come face to face with, in the days to come.

"Now, let's enjoy our meal and talk about details." Hal signaled the waiter who came and took their orders. "Two steaks with all the trimmings, please, my friend, and a fresh bottle." Hal looked at Jack for approval. Jack Bridger smiled and nodded in agreement.

"We'll take a cab home." They laughed.

Chapter 3

"I want you to meet my friend, tomorrow," Hal began as they tucked into their late night meal. "His name is Harry Langston. He's a Brit. Bit of an eccentric but very on the ball when it comes to this kind of thing. He has the *something* he wants to give us. I know him well and believe it or not, other forces are probably watching him to see just what he is up to. The object and the information he wants to hand over with it is, in his words, *dynamite*."

"So how do you know this guy?"

"Harry and I go back a long way. We met in church in the States when he was on holiday. He was into all kinds of conspiracy stories, and we really took to each other as friends. Besides his gift for making you feel he was reading your brain like yesterday's news, Harry was a very charming and quiet man. When he went home, we kept in touch."

"So you left the USA came to the UK and continued the friendship with Langston?"

"I carried on with the oil business for some years, went to night school, Bible college. Then we decided to start broadcasting across the USA with news we felt was relevant and not being adequately reported by the usual State controlled, or heavily influenced, news channels. Stacey and I sold up and came here to launch I.N.S. in the UK. That was when Harry contacted me a few months ago. He had read about I.N.S. starting up, saw my name and rang the office.

"Turns out Harry had progressed to joining the Freemasons and in the process became involved with some very nasty, influential people, you know, politicians and bankers, the powers that really pull the strings of different governments while kidding us the leaders we see on the newscasts really are the ones making the decisions, when much of the time it is the dastardly wicked and demonically directed people behind the scenes.

"Well, Harry became disillusioned with the people he was involved with and in the process came up with the idea of collecting as much information on these people and their plans as he could. Somehow, these people found out. They now want whatever he has, and they want it bad enough to kill him for it.

"Harry is a dedicated Christian, but he fell in with these people believing they were working for the good of humanity when in fact the opposite is true. He has a razor-sharp mind and sees things beneath the surface of world events others do not, yet even he was taken in, to begin with. By some underground contacts, he got a hold of a whole bag full of information. Harry says it is too hot for him to handle and wants us to have it. As well as the plans I outlined a moment ago; it concerns the new President of the European Union: Emmanuel Kohav.

"Harry intends to hand over all he has to us tomorrow. It's this plan I just told you about, and somehow Kohav is heavily involved.

"Apparently, these people have gone nuts and want Harry's head on a spike, but not before they know what he has done with the item and get it from him asap."

"Why don't they just threaten his family or beat it out of him?" Jack asked spreading out his hands.

"Wouldn't work. Harry has no family to speak of, and he is certainly no squealer. Also, his faith is so strong the threat of death means nothing to him."

"Okay, so where and when am I to meet this mysterious mister Langston and his *dynamite*?"

"You don't. Well, not officially anyway," Hal poured them both another glass of wine. "I want you to visit Westminster Abbey tomorrow. At precisely two thirty you will be standing beside the tombs of Queen Elizabeth the First and Queen Mary." Bridger interjected.

"Do I wear a buttonhole and carry a copy of the Times? That's what most spies do, don't they?" Hal was growing frustrated with Jack's skepticism. "I am deadly serious, Jack. The risks here are very real. Please understand this, or we end the meeting here, and I get Dave Miller to do the job."

"Miller?" Jack almost shot out of his seat. "Hal, I want this assignment more than ever now. Miller has been worming his way into my shoes since I arrived. I am not stepping aside for that journalistic opportunist. I am all ears and deadly serious. I apologize."

"Great, now I really do have your attention," Hal patted his mouth with the serviette.

"As I have already said, he is probably being watched. The moment he heads for the airport, seaport or any news outlet he's as good as dead. When you are in the Abbey mingling with crowds of tourists is the best time for him to hand it over."

"Couldn't he send it by Fed Ex?"

"Too dangerous. Come on, Jack. You know how posting even by Fed Ex is just as dangerous for something as important as this. If it falls into the wrong hands, it's game over for all of us. It needs to be delivered by hand."

"Okay, so how will I know him?"

"Don't concern yourself with that. He'll find you. You are to carry an umbrella. Place a red ribbon on the handle where it can be seen."

"Hal, do you really believe this Harry guy?" Bridger rubbed his chin.

"If I didn't trust him we wouldn't be having this conversation," said Hal. "He's scared witless. He says the information must be out of his hands tomorrow or he's afraid they will somehow get it from him." Jack felt shamefaced. "Hal, I apologize again for my poorly placed skepticism and disbelief. If you say you believe all this, I accept it though I do find the spooky part hard to swallow, even from you. But you're the boss. I promise to be careful and if this turns out as you suspect I'll do my darndest to get you the story that'll blow the ears off the world."

They shook hands across the table. Hal relaxed and smiled. "Okay, remember, tomorrow, Westminster Abbey, two thirty. Let's eat."

Chapter 4

The multi-storey car park in Great College Street was almost full as he searched for a good spot to leave the car. Harry Langston was a short man just under five feet seven. But that was a good point in his favor today. Today, he wanted to be short: short enough to pass among crowds unnoticed. Short enough to lose anyone who attempted to follow him as he made his way through the mass of tourists wandering around the ancient Cathedral in the center of London.

The site of Westminster Cathedral was originally a Benedictine Abbey, built around the year 960 AD and replaced by the present Abbey in 1245 when Henry III decided he wanted something grander.

Harry was proud of his English heritage: proud of the weight of history that hung over the city of London and this ancient building that housed the remains of seventeen monarchs, including Elizabeth the First and her half-sister Mary to whose shared shrine he was now heading.

He knew he was being followed when he left his home in St. John's Wood and set off for the city. It had been obvious as he drove away. The quiet lane very rarely saw any cars apart from those driven by the few residents who lived there or the regular delivery vans. But as he pulled into the main road, he glanced into his rearview mirror and noticed another car pull out of the lane and follow him. It followed him all the way into the city. "*A little too obvious: they want me to know they are on my tail*," he mused.

When he finally arrived and found a spot to park, the tail was nowhere to be seen. But as he left the building and came onto the street, he stopped to cross the road, looked over his shoulder and noticed a man leaving the exit behind him. As he glanced back their eyes met and he knew. The cold stare in the man's eyes told Harry all he needed to know.

Doing his best to become smaller than ever, he positioned himself deep among the crowd building up at the crossing. The tail stood at the back of the pedestrians waiting to cross, trying his best to keep his eyes on Harry's movements.

Crossing the road and taking a right turn he walked through the Dean's Yard and the Abbey's garden precincts, then moved quickly to the Cathedral and walked in among the throng, the tail still following close behind. He prayed to God today was a good day to be a short Englishman.

At that same moment, Jack Bridger had made sure he was on time, complete with umbrella and ribbon. Journeying into the city by train and then by tube he entered the ancient Cathedral and casually made his way around, doing his best to look as touristy as possible.

He wasn't used to the cloak and dagger way of getting a story, but he had decided *needs must*, and this was a story worthy of pursuit.

Passing the tombs of some of the great and some of the not so noble he finally sauntered toward the tomb of Elizabeth the First.

Elizabeth had also been the first female head of the Church of England following the death of her father, Henry the Eighth. She was entombed along with her Roman Catholic half-sister Mary, also known as "*Bloody Mary*" due to the three hundred plus Protestant martyrs she had burned at the stake during her reign.

"*Odd,*" thought Bridger. "*Rivals in life, companions in death.*"

He stood for a few moments reading the plaque bearing their names. Someone brushed against him.

"Jack Bridger, I presume?" the figure whispered.

Jack looked straight ahead. "And you are?"

"Harry. I do not have what you want with me. My address is now in your pocket."

Bridger's heart sank. "Is this a con. job? I am not here to be taken in on some fool's errand. Do you have the item or not?"

"At my home, in my study, where I feel safe to talk. It is not safe for me to carry the object out of my home."

"Are you kidding me?" Bridger felt his face redden with anger. "I traveled into town on the train for this secret spy nonsense rather than my car. Now I have to travel all the way home empty handed and start all over again another day. This is nuts. Totally nuts. And for what?"

"I had to be sure who I am dealing with. I am sorry, Mister Bridger, but I am telling you this information is vitally important." There was a short silence.

Harry continued."Come to my home this evening."

"But I'd take a guess if this is as earth-shattering as Hal suspects, your home is being watched: this is crazy."

"Correct, but the idiots only watch the front at present to see who is coming and going. My home is the only place in the lane with a red bricked wall on top of a high grassy bank.

"Come over the back wall to the rear of the building. I'll leave a window open at the back, on the ground floor. Come in and up the stairs to my study, first door on the right. I'll be waiting and give you what you need. But be aware, the information I will hand over to you is vital. Handle with the most exceptional care, and you must not under any circumstances share it with anyone other than Hal, and those immediately involved.

"Also, I cannot stress again, too strongly, that this information is of the utmost importance.
I have been a virtual prisoner in my own home since discovering this information. I contacted Hal and arranged this meeting. Since that time I haven't dared to leave the house. These swine know I have collected this information, and they've been on my tail for some time. Time is not on our side. I believe I'm a dead man walking. I apologize, but you, my friend, are in mortal danger from this moment on. Please, my home this evening before it is too late." He turned and walked away, lazily gazing at the other relics of English history as he melted into the crowd.

Jack continued to gaze at the tombs of the two Queens for a moment, wondering just what wild errand he had become involved in, then he too turned and followed Harry toward the exit, well behind but making sure his short frame kept in view.

Suddenly he noticed a scuffle up ahead and heard a popping sound. Someone screamed as Harry dropped to the floor out of sight. Bridger pushed through the crowd to find him lying face down and a man hurriedly going through his pockets. A stream of blood trickled from the side of Harry's body forming a small pool on the ancient flagstones.

Jack slid in front of the kneeling figure edging him away from the body. Their eyes met, and a look of fury crossed the stranger's face as he moved out of the way. Gently rolling Harry onto his back and cradling his head in the crook of his arm, Jack took hold of his hand as he shouted: "Someone call an ambulance."

Harry's eyes flickered open and seeing Jack his lips parted. Bridger leaned over him, placing his ear to the dying man's lips. "My inside pocket, car keys, use my car quickly. Ford Fiesta, third floor, Multi-storey, Great College Street."

"I know it," Bridger whispered.

"Get there before they do, for God's sake, for God's sake. Remember, Jack," His voice was barely audible. "A rose by any other name, a rose by any other name. Remember, Jack. Go quickly." His eyes closed and he gasped as if wanting to say more but fell limp.

Jack felt for his pulse but could find nothing. The blood was oozing through Harry's jacket as Jack opened it and tore open the shirt. A small, neat hole leaking blood sat in the middle of his chest.

Looking around Bridger caught sight of the stranger that had been kneeling beside Harry.

The man smiled at him. A cold, contented, satisfied smile. He turned and swiftly vanished among the onlookers.

Jack Bridger checked the pulse in Harry's neck, but all was still. Paramedics and police pushed their way through. Before they could grab Bridger and start asking questions, he slid back into the crowd and made his way to the exit.

As he stepped out into the sunlight, he spotted the man moving fast along Victoria Street toward Parliament square. He looked back and caught sight of Bridger in pursuit. Jack shouted. "That man! Stop him! Stop that man."

The chase was on. He sprinted across the road beside the statue of wartime leader Sir Winston Churchill, and toward Westminster Bridge spanning the river Thames. The man leaped down the stairs into Westminster underground station with Jack, now throwing caution, and the umbrella, aside in full pursuit.

People were everywhere, milling about buying tickets; walking; running; standing; talking to each other.

Forcing his way through the mass of bodies, the hunted man jumped over the ticket barrier, pelting down the escalator, pushing people aside in his bid to escape, with Jack on his heels following his every move.

The sound of an approaching train echoed through the tunnel as the two of them came running onto the crowded platform with Jack Bridger just fifteen feet behind his target.

The man was trapped, and he knew it. He came to a dead stop and swung around, facing Jack. Bridger stopped running and began walking purposefully toward him, his hands balled into fists ready to take the thug down.

But the man suddenly smiled and made a move toward him. Jack saw the shape of the gun the man was holding in his raincoat pocket.

"That was rather stupid, old chap," the thug, with a cultured voice, smiled.

"Should've let me walk. But as you are so keen

to meet me." he nodded over Jack's shoulder and a voice, calm and collected whispered "Here comes our train: move." The voice had a hand that held Bridger's bicep from behind like a vice.

"And if I don't, you'll shoot me here in front of all these nice people?"

"Don't get too smart, sir. We saw you give chase. Did you think we'd send just one man on the job? I followed you to the Cathedral. My colleague here followed the gentleman you met. I'm afraid you are in a lot of trouble, sir. We needed to get you away from the Abbey and the police. I knew you'd give chase down here right where we want you. You were so intent on following my colleague you didn't notice me running behind you. I'll have to ask you to accompany us on a short ride, quietly and without any fuss, if you please."

"But no one else knew I was going to the Abbey."

The train was pulling into the platform.

"Oh, really?" said the voice. "Now please do as we say. We don't want to cause a scene do we?"

The shape of the gun shifted, pointing to the train as it came to a halt. "All we want is whatever Langston gave you in the Cathedral, and we'd like to know what he said to you."

"Okay, okay." Bridger had no choice but to get on the train.

There was a crush of lunchtime commuters and tourists boarding the tube. Jack knew in a moment the doors would be closed and he would be trapped with the two Old Etonian type thugs.

They stuck close to him, but a heavily overweight businessman in suit and bowler pushed his way into the carriage, and for a moment Bridger was separated from them and found himself close to the opening.

"Please mind the doors" the robotic voice warned.

As the doors began to slide shut, Jack stepped forward onto the platform. He turned and saw the two men frantically trying to prise the doors open as the train moved away. He couldn't help but give them a grin and a mock salute tapping his forehead and raising his hand to wave. But his delight was short lived. A moment later the train came to a stop. They must have pulled the emergency cord.

The train doors opened, and a tsunami of people flooded across the concourse pushing, clawing one another in their panic.

Someone shouted, "There may be a bomb," and the tsunami increased in intensity, everyone screaming, pushing, punching, trying to squeeze onto the stairway to the street above.

Jack spotted the two men struggling to get to him through the crowd, but because the train had stopped farther down the track, they were a good fifty feet away, separated from him by a river of moving, shouting, crying bodies pushing them in the wrong direction toward the escalators.

A screaming woman ran into Bridger as she blindly headed toward the exit followed by others wanting to flee the scene.

The collision brought him to his senses. He could not follow the woman back the way he had come, or he would run right into the men who were now pursuing him.

His reporter's engine kicked in, and he knew in an instant he had to get to Harry's home before the mysterious people involved in his murder ransacked the place looking for whatever it was Harry had died protecting.

The police could wait.

Chapter 5

Jack Bridger spotted a service entrance about fifteen yards away, but it was in the wrong direction to the flow of people pushing him back toward the exit. He turned and with all his might went against the tide.

Managing to force his way to the entrance, he ran up the spiral stairs to the street, emerging into the sunlight of the Victoria Embankment.

He heard shouts and realized the two heavies had not given up the chase but were gaining, pounding up the staircase behind him.

He sprinted across the busy road beside the Tower housing Big Ben and ran for all he was worth along St Margaret's Street into Abingdon Street, turning sharply into Great College Street and the Multi-Storey car park in search of Harry's car.

Jumping into the lift, he pressed the button to the second floor. As he stepped out, he spotted a pile of traffic cones in a corner. Grabbing one, he quickly placed it in the lift doorway, preventing the door from shutting making sure his adversaries would have to use the stairs.

Taking Harry's car key ring from his pocket, he ran up and down the line of parked vehicles pressing the security fob. "C'mon C'mon."

A Ford Fiesta in the corner bleeped, and Jack ran, opened the door and jumped in.

Trying to drive at a speed that would not draw attention he exited the car park onto the street.

A few moments later a car appeared behind him on the ramp. He looked into his rear-view mirror.

It was them.

"Unbelievable," He swore out loud. "They must be athletes to have sprinted up the stairwell that quickly."

He pulled Harry's address from his pocket, switched on the SatNav, tapped it in and took off in the direction of Harry Langston's home and the object that had cost him his life.

Jack knew the people who had caused Harry's death now wanted his as well and would be watching Harry's house front and back. He glanced back down the street. They were still there, of course.

A little farther on Bridger noticed a parked police car: the officers sitting comfortably, idly watching the passing traffic. He slowed and wound down his window." Hey, officer," the policeman turned toward him. "Yes, sir?"

"Blue Mondeo five cars back nearly caused an accident back there. I think he overdid a lunch-time drink with the boys. He was all over the place. Someone needs to have a word before he causes a problem."

The officer rolled his eyes and sighed.

"Thanks, sir. Normal this time of day. We'll have a word." Jack nodded his thanks and picked up speed again. Looking in his rearview, he saw the officer get out of the police car and wave the Mondeo to a stop.

"That should hold them for a while." Jack grinned to himself.

Bridger quickly turned off the main street and pulled into a shopping mall. Driving around to the fifth-floor car park, he spotted a space almost hidden among over a hundred cars and slid into the spot.

Before leaving, he checked the glove compartment for anything useful. His hand felt a hard object. A torch. Shoving it into his pocket, he jumped out, quickly making his way toward the extensive array of shops. Once there he was about to call a cab on his cell phone but thought twice.

"Someone told those guys I would be at Westminster Abbey, so, are my calls being monitored or am I getting paranoid?" He mused.

He found a pay-phone and arranged to meet the cab at the service entrance.

Ten minutes later he gave the driver the address and was on route to Harry's home. Jack stopped the cab at the end of the lane and began to walk the remainder.

It was getting dark by now, and a light rain began to fall as he walked the deserted road. A cold wind began to rustle through the overhanging trees, shaking showers of droplets onto his head.

Harry's home appeared ghost-like through the windswept rain. It was now seeping through Jack's clothes as he trudged along, head down and shoulders hunched against the bitter wind and rain. As he walked, he had a few moments to review what had happened. If the people that had put a tail on him had any inkling of where he was going and why, someone could have gotten to the house before him and found what he was looking for.

Someone could be lying in wait for his arrival. Someone whose task would be to make sure he didn't leave on his own two feet.

As the house was set in its own grounds, he needed to make his entrance to the property as near the building as possible. Rather than go marching through the two massive wrought iron gates that formed the entrance, he did as Harry had ordered.

Slowly clawing his way up the bank beside the house he clambered over the high wall that surrounded the grounds. He landed on the other side, at the rear of the building among a pile of wet leaves someone had placed there for compost.

Moving swiftly, Jack found to his annoyance, though not to his surprise, all the lower windows were firmly locked.

"How the blazes am I to get in?" He screwed his eyes against the rain seeking some miracle of an opening and moved toward the far corner of the house as the wet seeped through his clothing, soaking his skin.

Wiping the rain from his eyes, he noticed two wooden doors on the ground almost hidden by grass and leaves.

"Thank God. A cellar!"

He kicked the debris away. The two iron handles were firmly in the embrace of a huge padlock. Jack knelt down and examined it. It was new but the handles it held in its grip were old and worn. Gripping both handles and gently pulling upward as far as the lock would allow he noticed one of the handles was coming away from the wood into which it had been screwed many years earlier. *"A couple of gentle tugs should do it."*

Heaving again, the wood splintered, and as he gently opened one of the doors, it let out a loud creaking sound, but no one came looking.

All was in total darkness as he slowly descended the dirty wooden steps to the cellar floor. It was now safe enough to bring the torch into play.

"Thanks, Harry," he spoke quietly into the darkness.

The torchlight revealed nothing but old tables and empty wine racks that looked as if they had not been used for decades. The weak light fell on a large wardrobe that probably had last seen daylight when Queen Victoria was a girl.

The whole place smelled of age and decay and the dust of decades floated across the beam as it cut through the darkness.

At last, he found a door and gingerly opened it half expecting someone to be waiting for him on the other side. It was tomb-like...quiet. He stopped and listened for any sound. Nothing but his heart pounding in his chest.

The stairs leading to the ground floor were narrow, and at the top, he could make out the outline of the door to the living area. It opened onto a large T shaped entrance hall. A lounge on his right, the dining room probably leading to the kitchen to his left and the front door directly ahead of him down the hall. To the left of the front door were the stairs leading to the first floor and presumably Harry's study.

Not wanting to spend any longer there than necessary, Jack headed for the stairs, figuring the study must be the obvious place he would find the prize he had come for. The thought infused more courage into him, driving him on with fresh determination. He mounted the stairs two at a time.

When he found the study, his heart almost stopped. The torch revealed a room that had been ransacked. Everything that could be opened, torn, thrown about the place, had been attacked unmercifully in the search for the prize.

He panned the torchlight. The place was a total disaster zone. The office desk was upside down; all its drawers were scattered around the room along with numerous books and papers. Even the paneling on the wall had been stripped in the search.

With his heart sinking, he realized he was too late. He lifted the upturned office chair, sank into it and hid his face in his hands in abject despair.

As he leaned back in the chair, gazing at the ceiling, a thought dawned on him.

"If they made this much of a mess, maybe they didn't find it after all."

With renewed energy he began to look around the room again, hoping whoever had been there had missed some little niche. But after a frantic ten-minute search, Jack once again sank into the chair, defeated.

Suddenly, he remembered Harry's dying words as he had tried to staunch the bleeding from the gunshot to his chest.

"Remember, Jack: a rose by any other name."

"What was he trying to say? Was it a coded message about the whereabouts of the object he was going to give me or was it simply the meaningless ramblings of a dying man?"

"Rose, rose." No new revelation came to him, and he was becoming more frustrated by the second.

"Was it in the rose bushes outside? Surely not." Leaning back and gazing up, his eyes focused on the light hanging from the ceiling.

"Rose… ceiling." He said out loud.

He sprang to his feet. "I wonder..." He recalled reading somewhere the ceiling rose was used as an emblem of secrecy during the rule of England's Tudor King, Henry VIII. The rose, suspended above a table, symbolized the freedom to speak plainly without repercussion and later became part of domestic architecture in ceiling light fittings.

"Why, Harry you crafty old Brit." Jack laughed out loud. Standing on the upturned desk, he gently unscrewed the light fitting in the ceiling.

"The rose...the ceiling rose. By any other name. What name? Secrecy. This study was where he said he could talk freely and secretly when we met on the ill-fated trip to London."

As he unscrewed the fitting, there was a click, and a panel opened in the ceiling. Jack slid his hand inside and felt around until he touched a small box. He managed to slip it toward the aperture, and it fell into his other hand. A small oblong box.

He clambered down and opened it.

A small flash drive lay on a velvet cushion. He closed the box quickly and pushed it into the inside pocket of his coat.

With an air of victory, he moved to make a fast exit.

As he did, he noticed a sudden raw chill had flooded the room. Jack opened the study door, but an invisible force wrenched the handle from his grasp as if he were a child. The door slammed shut with a report like a gun. He grasped the handle with both hands and turned it, but the door refused to budge.

Bridger stood frozen to the spot, unsure of what to do next.

He heard a movement.

Something was there with him in the dark, and the sudden awareness filled him with a chilling sense of foreboding.

The hairs on the back of his neck began to tingle, his legs grew weak, and despite the drop in temperature and the cold entering every pore in his body, he broke out in a cold sweat.

"Who's there?" he could see nothing.

Then the torchlight died, and the darkness closed in around him.

He desperately tried the door again, but it remained tightly closed as if it had been sealed shut.

Backing instinctively toward the wall, Jack could vaguely make out a form, steadily rising from the floor, outlined against the window.

It was accompanied by the most nauseating stench like that of rotting flesh. It filled his nostrils and almost made him retch.

The figure grew into a gigantic, naked man if one could call the creature a man. It stood with its bald head just inches from the ceiling.

Dark, violent eyes, set in a gray face,

narrowed as they set their sights on Jack who had now stiffened with a horror that riveted him to the floor. Its arms hung by its side. The fingers were crowned with long, claw-like nails.

Alone and unarmed, in a darkened room, Jack Bridger was confronted by something entirely beyond the range of his experience. A vile, malevolent being from a world beyond his own.

Jack's entire body was overcome, his veins felt as if they were filled with ice water. One thought filled his mind: this meant certain death. There was no possible hope of escape from this hideous demonic creature.

Bridger stood frozen with terror as the creature, emitted a low growl and began to move slowly and menacingly toward him.

Chapter 6

Bridger made a weak attempt to move toward the door, but the figure took a giant stride blocking his escape. As it did, it let out a low, menacing snarl. The creature was toying with him.

Jack stumbled back behind the upturned desk in a pitiful attempt to protect himself.

The beast's mouth opened, revealing gray-green teeth as the lips dripped saliva. "Come." The mocking, hollow sounding voice echoed through the room. Its horrid hands beckoned him.

"Come, come to me." it drooled in anticipation.

Jack felt faint; his head began to swim, as a feeling of complete exhaustion and nausea spread over him. He had an overwhelming urge to step toward the vile monster and surrender to his fate.

His foot took an involuntary step forward. Then another. He was moving as if he was an automaton under the control of an outside force. It was like a magnet drawing him. He could not resist even though his brain was screaming, warning him, this meant death, annihilation at the hands of this foul being sent from another dimension.

Until this moment Jack had relegated any idea of the supernatural to the world of fairy stories and old wives tales. But in one horrendous moment, it had become a terrifying reality.

He took another step and as he did his foot trod on one of the many books strewn around the room. Robotically he looked down. It was a Bible.

For the first time since childhood, he prayed, "God...help...me," barely able to speak, his voice croaked a plea to heaven.

"Jack, pick it up." A gentle voice, but full of authority, pierced his brain into sudden wakefulness.

"Jack, pick up the Bible."

A sudden surge of strength swept through his body as he swiftly took the volume in his hand.

Screaming with all his might, he flung the precious book into the face of the creature and cried, "In the name of Jesus Christ, I command you, return to the abyss from which you came."

As the Bible smashed into its face, the monster let out a wail of agony and stopped dead as if it had run into an invisible wall.

Its arms flailing, it made one last desperate swing toward Jack as it sank into the darkness.

For a few brief seconds, Bridger stood

transfixed, on the verge of vomiting as the creature's sickening odor continued to fill the room. His legs gave way, and he stumbled backward into the wall.

Picking up the precious book for protection he sprang to life and flung himself out of the room and down the stairs, not pausing to consider whether someone or something may be lying in wait for him.

Sprinting back down into the cellar and out again into the pouring rain, he ran to the wall and heaved himself up.

A hand gripped his foot. Looking down Jack saw the figure of a man in a hooded raincoat hanging on to him.

Panic-stricken, Jack kicked out violently with his free foot again and again into the man's face until it was a bloody mess and he felt the grip loosen.

The sound of running feet sounded along the alley beside the building. The man opened his mouth as if to call for help but one final kick under his chin sent him reeling onto his back.

The sound of more voices came from the front of the building and pierced the darkness.

They were everywhere, and they were after him.

Bridger threw himself over the wall, landed on

his back and rolled down the bank.

Picking himself up, still clutching the Bible, he began to run in stark terror toward the main road and the lights of civilization.

"God, help me. God, please help me" he kept repeating as he ran sobbing, half stumbling, half sprinting, toward the end of the lane.

He heard a sound behind him and looking over his shoulder made out the form of three men sprinting after him in the darkness.

As Jack came onto the main road, he was momentarily blinded as a car's headlights bore down on him and screeched to a halt. "Hello," said a familiar voice. "Thought you might need a lift. Hop in."

"Hal! Thank God."

Bridger jumped into the passenger seat and as the car began to move one of his pursuers caught up and smashed his fist through the side window, clawing at Hal's face. Hal let go of the steering wheel and grappled with the man who was now tearing at his face with one hand and trying to open the door with the other. The car veered across the road out of control. Jack leaned over, grabbed the wheel and pushed his foot hard on the accelerator.

There was a scream, and the car lurched and bumped as Hal's attacker lost his grip, stumbled and fell beneath the speeding vehicle.

"Hal," Jack gasped. "How the hell did you know I would be here?"

"How the heaven, you mean, my friend," replied Hal as he drove toward the darkened countryside.

"We picked up the news of the shooting at Westminster Cathedral. I knew at once, of course, you, Harry or one of the nefarious creatures that are bent on killing this information had to have been involved. Later webcam recordings showed you chasing the killer down into the underground. Witnesses stated Harry had fallen and you had come through the crowd to help. So you are more or less in the clear.

"Anyway, after seeing the news, I thought I had better drive out to Harry's and then to your place. Didn't have a clue what I was going to find or do when I arrived. I was just about to turn into the lane when you came flying out into my headlights with those guys behind you."

Bridger heaved a sigh. "Hal, I take back everything I ever, ever said to you about the supernatural. You were right, and I was so idiotically wrong. You won't believe what I have just experienced back there. I came face to face with something from another world." He was suddenly struck by the full force of events and the miraculous escape he had just made.

"Hal, stop the car." Hal pulled over and dabbed the blood oozing from the scratches he had received, while Jack stood by the side of the road and threw up several times, the creature's foul stench still in his nostrils.

After climbing back into the car, he found he could not stop shaking.

"Boss, I think I am going into shock."

"Tell me what happened back there?"

Bridger leaned his head back and slowly related the events of the last hour at Harry's house, pausing every few moments to take a few deep breaths. Gradually, the shaking stopped, and he was able to grasp what he had just experienced.

How I managed to get away from that foul, hideous creature, I don't know. I shouted words I have never uttered in my entire life. I can't even imagine where they came from."

"You say you heard a voice telling you to pick up the Bible?"

"Yeah, well, I think so. It was like I was in some half-waking nightmare where things appear real, but your head tells you they can't be. In ten minutes my whole belief system took a massive paradigm shift," He shook his head.

"Can't get my head around it. A voice told me to pick up the Bible. I did and then some, some power, a strength that wasn't mine, filled me and I shouted words I have never uttered up to that moment. I threw the book at that monster and, and..." As he relived the scene, he put his face in his hands and began to sob uncontrollably.

"Boss I thought I was going to die," He blurted between sobs. "Not just die, but I was about to be dragged off to God knows what world that thing came from. I have never been so scared.

"I don't know who how or why, but someone, God, Jesus, I don't know, but someone saved me." His face was deathly white, and his dry, ivory colored lips quivered with emotion.

Hal was silent for a few moments. The hum of the engine and the swish, swish of the wipers fighting the rain were almost comforting as they drove through the darkened lanes into the English countryside. Jack wiped his face with his sleeve and gradually regained his composure.

Hal spoke, "Jack, what you met was no nightmare, but a living, breathing creature from another dimension: a spiritual dimension inhabited by Satan and his demonic hordes.

"God spoke to you and saved you at the most dangerous moment of your life as you came face to face with a satanic entity. We'll talk about this later when you have rested. Now I want you to go straight to bed when we get to my home in Five Oaks."

"Your home? No. boss. I need to get home to my wife and some normality."

"Jack, Jack, think about it. That's a bad idea. We need to get you and Marsha to a safe house.

The people who are after the information we now have will stop at nothing to retrieve it. First, we'll collect Marsha then get her to Five Oaks. Once there we can think seriously about a safe house for us all. These people mean business and will not stop until we are silenced, and they have the item."

"You have it, I hope?"

Bridger patted his pocket. "Yeah, right here. I thought your pal would have it at the Cathedral."

"And he didn't?"

"No. That's why it was me you ran into back there. I had to get to Harry's after he was shot by whoever it is we are up against. He's dead, Hal. Shot right in front of me and hundreds of others. I went to the house, found a box, a flash drive inside, met that creature and ran. But I don't understand. That foul smelling being, and..." Once again, he relived the encounter with the being from the pit and began to shake. Hal laid a reassuring hand on Bridger's shoulder.

"Okay, Jack. Let's talk later," without taking his eyes off the road ahead; he tossed his cell phone to Jack's lap. "Here, if you are up to it you'd better call Marsha and tell her to pack essentials only."

Bridger dialed home, took a deep breath and trying to sound as calm as possible, briefly explained to Marsha what had happened, but without relating the story of the demonic encounter.

"We'll be there soon so pack essentials and be ready to leave when we arrive. I love you."

"But what is this all about, Jack?"

"Long story, Honey. I'll explain when we are together. Whatever you do, do not open the door to anyone…understand? I love you."

"Okay," she sighed. "I love you too. See you soon. Hurry." Marsha pressed disconnect and ran to the bedroom.

Turning the light on and pulling a case from the cupboard she opened the wardrobe and hastily packed a few items of clothing.

As she was collecting shaving gear, toothpaste other personal items from the bathroom, she thought she heard a sound downstairs.

Marsha froze.

"Hello? Is someone there? Jack, is that you?"

Another sound. This time a definite squeak of the door handle to the kitchen.

"Oh please God, no! The kitchen leads to the garden. Did I leave the garden door unlocked?"

Then a creak as somebody placed a foot on the first step on the staircase. Marsha knew those sounds by heart. Jack and she had always joked that they knew where each of them was in the house by the different sounds they had grown so used to. But now those same sounds became warnings: sirens screaming at her to get out. But she was trapped in her own home. She couldn't get out because someone was slowly coming up the stairs; coming for her.

Chapter 7

Marsha Bridger tiptoed from the on-suite back into the bedroom and quietly opened the wardrobe and tried to hide behind the clothing still hanging there. It was a pretty futile attempt even though it was a large piece of furniture and she hoped she could conceal herself in the darkness. She gently pulled the door shut and held her breath.

The intruder was on the landing. Then a man's voice began singing in a mocking tone.

"Marsha, Marsha come and play. I'll have some fun with you today."

Marsha wanted to scream, to run, but whoever was in her home was right outside the door of her bedroom, laughing, taunting her and singing.

"One potato, two potatoes, three potatoes, four. Will the lovely Marsha be behind this door?" He kicked the bedroom door with such violence, it crashed into the wall, leaving a small crater in the plaster.

Terrified, she bit her bottom lip so hard she thought she would draw blood at any moment.

"Oh, Marsha. You are a naughty girl. I'm getting warm, aren't I? Closer, closer, warmer, warmer." He began to shout. "Warmer, warmer, hotter, hotter, very hot, very hot, burning, burning, burning."

The wardrobe door flew open. Hands began to throw the clothing to and fro gradually inching nearer and nearer. She tried to stifle a scream as she forced herself further into the darkness away from those grabbing, clawing, searching hands.

A hand brushed against her foot and stopped.

"Ah, what have we found here in the dark?" The man grabbed her ankle, and Marsha exploded, screaming, clawing at the air and kicking as she was mercilessly dragged feet first onto the bedroom floor banging her head on the wooden flooring as she emerged into the light.

She was thrown onto her stomach, a gag was pushed into her mouth, and a hood was forced over her head. Her hands were drawn painfully behind her and tied making it almost impossible to move.

Then her kicking feet were tied together. The man lifted her as if she were a sack of trash and threw her over his shoulder.

"Be a good girl and don't struggle. You scream and fight, you die. Get it?"

She began to sob with fear and anger, gasping for breath as he carried her down the stairs, toward the garden door into the rain and the cloaking darkness of the night.

As he moved into the kitchen something hit him in the face with the force of a sledgehammer, and he and Marsha went down in a crumpled heap. Marsha began to scream and fight as hands lifted her to her feet. The hood came off, and she found herself looking into Jack's face.

"It's okay, honey. You're safe."

She fainted into his arms.

Bridger untied Marsha's bonds, carried her into the lounge and laid her on the settee. "My God, what have we got into?" Jack let out a hoarse whisper. Hal appeared at the kitchen door and stepped over the unconscious body of Marsha's assailant. "My dear young friend, we must keep cool heads. It appears these brutes were in the process of kidnapping Marsha in the hope we would exchange the flash drive for her life."

"Her life?" Jack exclaimed. "Who are these people? This is England. This doesn't happen here. What the heck is going on?"

Hal began to reply, but Jack cut him short.

"Look, Hal, I don't entirely know what is going on here, but it seems we have fallen into a pretty unlawful game and I want no part of it.

"The way I see this, off the top of my head, the ones who killed Harry and tried to snatch me also found out where I live have now come to my home and attempted to take Marsha. All we need to do is contact the police, tell them everything, and clear up this whole mess. Your friend has dragged us into God knows what and it cost him his life."

"Yes, Jack, I am certain the people who killed Harry are the same people who were at his home and who have just attempted to snatch Marsha. In God's good grace we arrived in the nick of time. They were going to use her as a bargaining chip in exchange for whatever is on the flash drive."

Bridger whispered as if to himself, "Oh my Lord, we even ran one over as we bolted in the car. We may have killed a man. What is going on? Let's go now to the police. We are wasting time."

Before Hal could answer, they heard a movement from the kitchen. Jack ran to the room in time to see Marsha's assailant sprinting across the garden to the lane at the rear of the house leaving a trail of blood behind him. Jack gave chase but was too late. The man leaped into a van and sped off into the darkness.

Bridger walked back into the house and a moment later his cell phone rang. Lifting it from his pocket, he saw it was an unregistered number.

"Hello?"

"Mister Bridger?" the voice had a cultured British accent.

"I understand I must congratulate you on the splendid rescue of your lovely wife?"

"Who is this?" Jack's voice trembled with emotion as he put the phone on speaker so Hal could listen.

"That shouldn't concern you," the voice continued.

"My associate has just informed me of your heroism in saving your wife. I understand his face is in an awful mess. The reason I am calling is to give you some helpful advice toward preventing any such experience occurring in the future."

For a moment Bridger was silent.

"Mister Bridger? Are you still there?"

"Go on," Jack's nerves were stretched to breaking point.

"Well, let me see. The first piece of helpful advice is to dissuade you from going to the police or making any other ridiculous moves."

Jack exploded. "Do you really think you can

get away with this? If you do, you are an imbecile. Supposing we go to the police right now and tell them what we know?"

"Bridger, please wake up. What do you know? We are beyond the law! We can very easily see to it you are laughed out of any court in the land. You, my dreamy headed friend, will be viewed as an overzealous reporter who concocted a wild conspiracy theory after seeing his friend shot and murdered in a cowardly attempted robbery gone wrong. You will be seen as a low life opportunistic out for a sensational story by feeding on the tragic murder of your friend."

Jack felt the blood drain from his face. "You scum."

"Sticks and stones, sticks and stones. Don't be so naïve, Bridger. It has been done in the past with persons who were far more in the public eye than you, and it can easily be achieved in the case of some obscure TV personality trying to make a name for himself if you'll pardon me for hurting your already overblown ego.

"We can make any or all of you simply disappear, Mister Bridger. All we require is the flash drive, and you can carry on with your lives intact. If you attempt to share its contents, we'll see to it you and those you care about will suffer. We have the power to bury any information you try to pass on to others. We'll see to it you get buried as well. Do I make myself clear?"

"Well, you are going to be hard-pressed to find us after tonight's little fiasco, chum," Jack responded. "So we'll see what people think when we blast your plans for the planet all over the news."

"Mister Bridger, you are most amusing," the voice let out a prolonged laugh.

"We have methods, of which you can barely dream. So it is utterly pointless to think you can run and hide from us." The voice turned suddenly serious.

"Now, we need the flash drive. We know you have it and I am sure you are aware there are certain avenues at our command we can utilize to help you make the correct decision," he paused. "Including forces other than the physical, as you, no doubt experienced earlier this evening. You are all out of bluffs.

"I'll let you think about it or...well; we'll see what other little surprises we can send to persuade you. Remember, it is impossible to hide from us." He chuckled. "Until later then, bye for now."

Chapter 8

Jack slammed the cell phone down on the table and ran his hands through his hair. "What on earth are we supposed to do, Hal?"

Hal let out a sigh and thrust his hands out in surrender. "Jack, I don't know. I simply do not know what to do. On the one hand, I fear that unless we cave in to their demands, our lives and the lives of those we love will be in extreme peril and there is practically nothing we can do about it."

"Well of course," said Jack. "We must give these swine what they want. We don't even know what if anything is on the flash drive. There's no way I am about to hold onto to the drive and let you, Stacey and my wife run the risk of being murdered for whatever is on it.

Let them play their games of world conquest. At this moment all I want is to get out of this mess. It's too big for a little company like ours, Hal."

Hal gripped Jack by the shoulders. "But you must realize we are involved in something that is infinitely more important than we can ever imagine: more important than any of us. We are in it now, and there is no way we can walk away, even if we want to. I told you last evening there are evil, physical and spiritual forces at work here. Earlier today, you witnessed a sample of the power they possess in that they are capable of summoning up the foul creature you encountered. I do not doubt that these swine, as you rightly call them, having committed murder just hours ago, will not think twice when it comes to sacrificing any of us to get their hands on the information we now have in our possession."

"Then give them what they want." Jack was almost beside himself as he shouted into Hal's face. Hal gripped Jack's shoulders even tighter and shook Him. Then, looking directly into his tear filled eyes he said

"My friend, you are not thinking straight. You know how these people work. There is no way they will not carry out their threats regardless of whether we give them what they want or not. They hold all the cards at the moment, and we are holding a dead hand."

Jack took in a deep breath, "Hal, I know you are right...I know. Just don't want to even think about it. But what else can we do?"

"We must find a way to fight them. We can't just roll over. Whatever is on the flash drive is important enough to kill for."

Jack nodded and smiled grimly. "I understand

what you are saying, Hal, but that is the tough Texan oil man turned reporter in you."

Hal responded, "Jack, if we stand any hope of getting the upper hand over these people we need to coldly and soberly, take whatever steps are necessary to, first of all, find out what is on the drive." He paused, then added "Of course, there is a slim chance they would just fade away if we gave them what they want. But that is about as likely as six feet of snow in the Florida Keys. It's obvious we simply can't take that chance. We must find out what is on the flash drive. It's our only bargaining chip. Even if we said we don't know what it contains they'd probably kill us anyway, just in case we were lying."

Bridger sighed. "I see your point, Hal. You are correct, of course. But how do we go about deciphering the contents? That's the rub."

Hal nodded in agreement. "Well, thank goodness I have an old friend, we need to get to, Jack. Let's quickly get to his safe house where I'll tell you all I know and believe me it will blow your mind. I am so sorry I got you into this. I knew the dangers but for some reason never saw it spilling over into murder and attempted kidnapping all in one day."

"I know you didn't intend it to get so out of

hand, Hal. But it has, and you are right, we must quickly formulate some battle plan against these people. But in the meantime, what do we do? We don't even know who they are."

"It's obvious they believe Harry told you where the drive was hidden before he died. And that was why you went immediately to the house instead of to the police after his murder."

"So, now what? Go to the police? I guess that's out," Jack answered his own question.

"We don't dare. These guys must be aware of the dreadful position they have placed us in. The moment they feel there is any hint of police involvement they will put their power plan into play. Over time we will be made to vanish. Either they will invent some fake news story that will incriminate the company and us or they could make one of us appear to commit suicide as a taster of what they are capable of doing to persuade us to cave in.

"My guess is they are part of the secret elite Harry was always warning me about. Extremely secret, and unbelievably powerful, they are part of the behind the scenes movers and shakers of the world. The government behind the government. No matter what we tell anyone only the truth seekers and conspiracy crew would believe our story, and there are not many in the shadow governments of the world willing to blow the whistle on their masters."

Jack hung his head, the knowledge that their lives depended on whatever moves they made in the next hours and days was almost too much to bear.

"Yeah, I understand. I always thought the so-called elite only existed in the minds of idiotic conspiracy theorists with nothing better to do with their lives. Now I am beginning to see the world from a different perspective. So we wait?"

"We take time out, and we plan." The elderly American released Jack's shoulders and put his arm around him.

Marsha was slowly coming around, and Jack knelt beside her, stroking her hair away from her face.

"What happened," groaned Marsha and put her hand to her forehead. "Jack, Jack, that man," she whimpered and threw her arms around her husband's neck. She suddenly became angry.

"Just where is he? I'll break his nose for him."

"It's okay, honey. I beat you to it with a garden spade. He's gone back to his bosses, carrying what's left of his nose with him. How are you feeling? We need to be on the move in case they come back."

Marsha gingerly swung her legs off the settee and with Jack's arm around her slowly stood to her feet. She noticed Hal in the doorway.

"Why, Hal. I didn't see you there," she mumbled through her confusion. "What's all this about? What was that man doing in our home trying to kidnap me?"

Jack Bridger held her close and guided her toward the doorway. "Marsha, darling, we are involved in some very grave business, but we should be on the move: Hal and I will explain everything as we go."

Hal nodded. "They probably haven't gone to my home yet as it is you, and what you hold, they are after. But I'll ring Stacey, get her to pack a few things and get out at once. I know exactly where to go. Let's get your essentials."

After quickly finishing packing their bags, Jack and Marsha followed Hal back to the car.

Hal looked at his young friends as he buckled up. "Take heart, Jack, and Marsha. You may not believe it, but God really is on our side on this one. We will find this vile little group, and I promise you, my friends, all the demons in Hell, not even Satan himself, will stop us."

They took off at speed, winding through the country lanes, the headlights cutting through the darkness and the pouring rain, myriads of liquid pellets splattering against the windshield. Time was now of the essence, and they had not a moment to lose. Hal keyed in his home number and placed the phone in its receptacle beside him so he could be hands-free. Giving Stacey a brief rundown of events, he said: "Stace, you know our friends who invited us last week to come and stay with them?"

"Of course. You mean..."

Hal cut her off, "No names, Stace. Understand? Don't call them from where you are or on your cell. Just get in the car and go. Pack what you can for the two of us. Make sure you are not followed. Okay, darling? But please, call me when you are on your way, and I'll see you there. Now please, for your own safety, do as I ask and move, now." Hal emphasized the last word.

"Okay," she replied. "But there's something I think you should know."

"Can it wait until we meet?"

"I guess so. From the way you are talking it's something I can't really share with you over the phone right now."

"Right. Just move and do it fast. As long as you are okay, anything else can wait."

"It can, but I think you need to hear what I have to say as soon as possible."

"We shouldn't be too long. See you soon." He ended the call and turned to Jack, "I thought it would be better if we went straight to the safe house. That way Stacey doesn't need to wait for us."

"Good idea, Hal," Jack mumbled. His mind was in a fog: a living nightmare. In one day he had witnessed a murder, chased the murderer and been chased in return, had an encounter with a creature from another world and now rescued his own dear Marsha from being kidnapped.

He gazed blindly ahead into the tree-lined road ahead, lit by the car's lights.

Suddenly he was wide awake, "Hal, slow down: what's that up ahead?"

Hal leaned forward, straining to see what it was that was forming in front of them. He slowed down and peered over the steering wheel into the darkness.

What had initially appeared to be a small wall of mist above the trees began to change color until it became a huge, red, pulsating ball, impenetrable even with the car headlights full on.

Like a living thing, the revolving mass began

to move swiftly toward them. Marsha let out a terrified scream as Hal pulled the car to a screeching halt and said, "I've heard of this kind of thing when I was in the occult, and I'm telling you if that foul entity reaches us it's game over. Someone wants us dead and has conjured this up to finish us off. We have to get away from it immediately."

Jack shouted, "Reverse, man, reverse."

Hal swiftly changed gears, then floored the pedal. For a moment the wheels spun on the wet asphalt, then found their grip. The car flew backward with the red globe in pursuit.

With hedgerows on either side, it was impossible for them to turn off the road.

The red mass grew ever larger until it seemed to engulf the whole width of the road. As the car gathered speed so did the ball, only faster until it was almost towering above them.

"Hal, it's almost on top of us. Faster man, faster for God's sake. What is it? "

Hal was too busy looking over his shoulder watching the road behind. He spotted a small turn off and took it. The car lurched as it shot into a field and came to a bone-shuddering halt, the rear wheels sinking into the sodden ground.

"Lord God, help us," Hal shouted, looking to

the heavens. "Jack, Marsha get a firm grip on one another. Get out of the car and run for your lives, run now!"

Chapter 9

They ejected from the car into the pouring rain, sinking up to their ankles in the mud. The ball-like entity seemed to have a life of its own and passed through the trees onto the field behind them. As it moved through the trees, all the foliage withered and died and the branches fell limp.

Hal looked around in despair. He knew they were as good as dead if the globe overtook them. Already they could feel themselves growing weak as its outlying mist began sucking strength and life itself from their struggling bodies. Their heads started to pound in tune with the throb of the towering mass above them.

Running through the pouring rain and the thick mud made every step more painful, more draining for them.

"Church," Hal panted, his words coming in short gasps. "The church...over there." The muscles in his throat ached with the strain of speaking. The desire to just lay down in the mud and sleep was almost overwhelming.

Jack could make out the form of a church about fifty yards from them.

"Can't make it," he gasped.

Marsha lost her shoes in the mud and tried to sprint, but every muscle in her body seemed paralyzed while the two men gasped for breath and staggered as if they were about to collapse.

Hal shouted, "We must run, or we're dead." He felt as if his heart was about to burst in his chest.

The two men threw their arms around Marsha's waist and forced themselves to move through the pain of lifting each foot as the three of them made a last desperate effort to reach the safety of the hallowed ground, literally pulling each other along.

They stumbled into the ruin: the remains of an ancient Norman church built in the 11th century following the conquest of England by King William of Normandy in 1066. But, ruined though it was, it was erected on holy ground, dedicated to God many centuries ago. Now it offered heaven's protection to three fugitives from evil almost a thousand years later. They stumbled through the crumbling arched doorway.

"Quick to the altar, Jack, Marsha. The altar." Hal rasped, his throat sore and dry from the effort of trying to speak.

Finding their strength slowly returning they threw themselves against the ruined high altar.

The altar and the remains of the surrounding walls were covered in moss and dirt, but they didn't care. The rain swept through the ancient windows now broken and open to the elements; the stone-slabbed floor lay covered in weeds and mud.

They laid there, drawing sharp breaths, looking up through the open roof at the sky, as the rain pelted down on them.

The blood colored globe of evil seemed to surround the ruin, but could not penetrate the walls to reach them. An accompanying howling wind swirled and buffeted the walls as if trying to throw them to the ground, but without success. The loose debris was swept up as if in a whirlwind, hitting their faces.

Hal laid his hands on his friend's heads and at the top of his voice began to recite Psalm Ninety one.

"He that dwelleth in the secret place of the most High shall abide under the shadow of the Almighty. I will say of the LORD, He is my refuge and my fortress: my God; in him will I trust. Surely he shall deliver thee from the snare of the fowler, and from the noisome pestilence. He shall cover thee with his feathers, and under his wings shalt thou trust: his truth shall be thy shield and buckler. Thou shalt not be afraid for the terror by night; nor for the arrow that flieth by day; Nor for the pestilence that walketh in darkness; nor for the destruction that wasteth at noonday..."

As he recited the Psalm, the globe began to dissipate slowly and the wind faded.

Hal shouted, "Praise you, oh Lord God, King of the universe. You are above all the gods and king over all the elements. The gods of the heathen are demons. All will fall and confess you as Lord. Thank you, Lord, for your miraculous deliverance today. You have rescued Jack from the manifestation of the demonic and Marsha from being kidnapped. And tonight you have again stretched out your hand and saved the three of us from certain death. Please, Lord, protect our loved ones tonight. Guide us and give us your wise counsel as to what we should do in the coming days. Grant us courage and power through the Holy Spirit. We ask these things and thank you with all our hearts in Jesus' name. Amen."

When he had finished praying the rain began to turn to a light drizzle and the globe that had so nearly engulfed them and caused their end, faded. In another moment it had gone entirely.

"That was as close as I ever want to come to evil." Hal gasped.

They lay there caked in mud and moss for a few minutes as their strength returned.

"What was that?" spluttered Marsha her eyes wide with fear as she pushed her back against the altar in search of further protection.

"In my occult days, I heard of that kind of thing only once when it supposedly sucked the very lifeblood from a man our leader had cursed. So, from what I had been told, I recognized it at once," said Hal. "Never have I felt so close to death as tonight. Whoever they are behind the murder of Harry, your encounter with that creature at his home and the attempted abduction of Marsha, I would hazard are also very powerful practitioners in the Black Arts: Black Magic, if you will. It's obvious they are very much in contact with the dark side.

"They summoned that deadly manifestation to finish off the three of us. But God has other plans." He paused, then said "Let's move. We'll try and get the car back on the road."

"What about that thing that just chased us?" asked Jack.

"I believe we shall be okay now, but we had better get a move on just in case. Anyway, we can't stay here forever. We need to get to the safe house."

Picking themselves up they made their way out of the building that had helped save their lives only moments before. Jack and Marsha quietly followed Hal like children unsure of where they were being led.

They reached the car and found one rear wheel had hit a rock in the field just below ground level. It was this that had prevented their reversing any farther off the road, and the car had not sunk as deep into the mud as they had feared.

With Marsha at the wheel and Jack and Hal pushing from behind they were surprised and relieved to find after a few minutes of rolling back and forth, the car suddenly revved up and out onto the solid tarmac of the road. The men climbed back in. Marsha climbed into the back with Jack.

Hal said, "I hope this shows you, my friends, we are up against some deadly adversaries. People who will not stop before they have the information we hold, or we are dead before being able to do something with it."

Jack frowned, "But what is on the flash drive?"

"That, Jack, is the sixty-four thousand dollar question. I don't know for sure, but the fact that our friend Harry was willing to die to protect the information it contains, makes it obvious what we have in our possession must be of stupendous significance. Also, as I told you last evening, it involves Emmanuel Kohav. I have strong suspicions regarding that man, which I haven't shared just yet. When we get to the safe house, we will find out for sure."

His cell rang. It was Stacey calling in to let him know she was on her way.

"I left about thirty minutes ago and should get there within the hour," She said. "Is everything okay with you three?"

Hal screwed his eyes as he drove and looked down at the hands-free. "Yes, we are fine. Had a slight mishap but we are okay and on our way." Hal thought it better to explain what had just happened when he met Stacey later rather than go through the experience now.

"Did I hear someone cough as you spoke earlier?"

"That's what I need to tell you," She replied.

"Who's there with you, Stacey?" A note of alarm crept into his voice.

"It's Lauren, Hal. She came to the house earlier. She's sitting here beside me and is terrified of something. She says she'll only speak to you and Jack. So I had to bring her with me. She refused to leave me: even clung to me and begged me to let her come along as well. Hold on."

Lauren Hutton, Hal's private secretary, came on the line, "Hal, Hal," she began to sob.

"Hal, Jack, Marsha I am so sorry. I need to see you really urgently." Bridger and Hal glanced at each other. Hal said, "Lauren, are you okay?"

"I have information about the people you are up against."

Jack sat upright. "How do you know about them, Lauren? Has anyone contacted you?"

"Can't tell you everything on this line. But you must understand one thing."

"What is that? Please Lauren what is it you know? How do you know them?"

"I'll tell you everything I know when we meet, but first get rid of your cell phones. They can track you through the cells. Stacey and I will do the same when we hang up." Lauren's voice began to tremble with fear.

"Jack, these people are led by crazed maniacs: maniacs who are operating at the highest levels of world government. They want whatever it is your friend had." She began to cry again, and between the sobs, she said "I found out they worship the Devil. I know it sounds crazy, but in the next few months, they are planning to bring in the reign of the man Christians call the

Antichrist and whatever your friend had may help expose them. They will stop at nothing to get it. Not even murder."

Chapter 10

The large manor was set back in its own grounds, protected by a security team of ex-military and police. All of them misfits in their former professions, but physically able and sufficiently morally corrupt, to serve the New World Order.

Lord Francis Haldane sat behind his oak desk drumming his fingers on the green leather of his chair. The room was small compared to many others in the house, but it suited his sole purpose, and that was to be a part of the coming world government under the leadership he and his kind before him had worked unceasingly toward producing.

Now, they were on the verge of creating the major crisis Rockefeller had spoken of back in 1980 when he said: "All we need is the right major crisis and the world will accept the New World Order."

The time was ripe, and Haldane and his fellow elites were in no mood to allow some American TV magnet and his cronies to kill the plan by exposing it to the world before they were ready. At fifty-five years old and the latest Lord in the history of the Haldane family he had been automatically elected head of his section of the ultra-secret Committee for Global Governance on the death of his father ten years earlier. He knew all the secrets and where all the bodies of those who opposed the cabal were buried.

The shamefaced man standing before the desk hung his head, not daring to speak or look Haldane in the face.

"So, where are they now?" Haldane growled.

"Sir, we are not sure, but we believe they are somewhere in the South of England, possibly heading into Sussex. As I am sure you are aware, sir, the committee called upon the alien forces to destroy them, but Montgomery and his friends somehow managed to reach a ruined church and call on their God."

The aged Lord looked up from his desk and removed his glasses. "We are not sure, possibly and somehow they managed, are not the replies I was looking for."

"It's the best we have at present, sir. Harris is..."

Haldane slammed his fist on the desk and cut him short."Harris is a fool. He had one simple task: get the woman and bring her to us as a bargaining chip for the flash drive," He stormed, his voice at screaming pitch. "He failed. The committee does not take kindly to such failures."

"In his defense, sir, he was taken by surprise by her husband and his boss. If he had left with the girl a few minutes earlier ..."

"But he didn't, did he? He was told to take Carswell along with him as a look-out and as an apology for their catastrophic blunder in the Abbey killing and subsequent tangle with Bridger. We told Harris to follow at a distance to see what transpired between Langston and Bridger. But he took it into his head to kill Langston in full view of a few hundred witnesses. He was caught in the act of searching Langston's pockets and then made a run for it and led Bridger to Carswell, which I grant was a good move. They could have brought him here. But even that failed when he escaped. They then took off chasing Bridger to the house and even failed miserably to secure him there. We were forced to use the power of Lord Lucifer to summon a demon against Bridger but the cursed Messiah of God rescued him. After all that, Harris still thought he knew better than the Committee. He left Carswell twiddling his thumbs and went solo to get the woman." He gazed down at the desk, then lowered his voice and said abruptly, "Harris is of no further use to us: Carswell too. Both of them are useless loose cannons we cannot allow to continue. Bridger and his boss both saw their faces: they could easily be identified at some time in the future, and that would land us in the mire for sure. See to it they vanish."

"Do you mean...?"

"Do I have to paint a picture for you, Jenkins?" He slammed his fist on the desk again. "Those complete fools have placed us all in danger of exposure. I have to answer to the Committee and especially to President Kohav. We operate under the strictest secrecy beyond any government agency or black ops anywhere. This ridiculous blunder has threatened to expose us and our plans at any moment. When I say they are to vanish, I mean precisely that. No mistakes.

"In clear language: I want them dead, all identification, dental records, fingerprints, everything destroyed, burned, cremated and the ashes securely scattered in the English Channel. Is that clear enough? See to it within the hour. Now get out."

Chapter 11

Hal drove through the night as Jack and Marsha sat in the back and gave in to their aching bodies and traumatized minds, finally falling into a deep sleep. Marsha's head slowly slid from Jack's shoulder onto his chest.

They woke an hour later as they crossed the Sussex border heading toward the coast. Jack blinked his eyes in an effort to become more aware and asked, "Where are we now?"

"Sussex. Not far from the safe house where we can hopefully take a look at the information on the flash drive."

Bridger rubbed his aching neck. "Any idea what we'll find?"

"Well, as I said earlier, it cost Harry his life protecting it. After listening to Lauren it's only cemented my conviction, we have bitten into something incredibly evil and dangerous. Dangerous not only to us, but we may be in possession of something that carries eternal consequences to every man, woman, and child on the planet. If as Lauren says, it involves, the higher elite of world government and as Harry suggested President Kohav is in their plans for the rise of Antichrist, we may have just grabbed the tail of a proverbial demonic tiger."

They drove on in silence, through the Sussex countryside, deep in thought, passing through small villages devoid of street lights. The house lights were also extinguished, the inhabitants safely tucked up in their warm beds, unaware of the drama that was unfolding in the lives of the travelers passing through their streets.

Presently, as they drove back out into the darkened country along a tree-lined lane, Hal said: "We're here."

He swung the car off the road onto a large field, following a narrow track toward the rim of a valley on the far side.

The rain had stopped, and from their vantage point, they could see the moon behind the broken clouds, casting a silver stream of light upon the English Channel in the distance.

Reaching the edge of the field, the track suddenly dipped down the side of the valley. At the bottom, a cottage came into view, almost hidden among the trees.

The car came to a sliding halt in the mud beside the front door. Just ahead of them, they could see Stacey's car parked at the far end of the cottage and another just ahead of it. The front door opened and a stream of golden light shone out as Jack, Hal, and Marsha emerged from the car looking worn and bedraggled.

Silhouetted in the glow stood a figure of a young woman. "Hal. I am so glad you made it. Come on in." The voice was soft and warm, possessing a slight American twang.

"Dinah, my dear." Hal almost lifted the girl from her feet as he hugged her then realized he was still caked in dry mud and quickly let her loose.

"You don't know what your kindness tonight means to us." He said, holding both her hands in his.

Dinah Goldberg led the trio inside. "I'm beginning to get an idea," she smiled. "Take off your coats and shoes: ah, I see Marsha has none. No worries, I am sure we'll find out why." She smiled comfortingly.

"Come into the lounge. You must be hungry, so Stacey and I are preparing supper." She stopped and looked them up and down, noticing their muddy clothes and faces.

"You can all take a shower, and we have some spare clothes too, and even shoes for Marsha: we look about the same size…if you are interested? But I guess you have bought extra clothing just as Stacey has for her and Hal?" she said to Jack and Marsha who nodded.

The three smiled, and Hal introduced Jack

and Marsha as Stacey ran from the kitchen into Hal's arms, hugging him and kissing his muddy cheek. She let out a gasp when she saw the wounds on his face.

"It's okay, honey. Just a few scratches. You should see the other guy."

Hal pulled himself away from his wife for a moment and over her shoulder addressed a tall, thin man with a slightly balding head of rust-colored hair.

"Aaron, thank you so much for this. Let me introduce my friends: Jack Bridger and his wife Marsha," he said, nodding toward the bedraggled couple who were thanking Dinah for her hospitality.

They shook hands as Aaron Goldberg removed his glasses and said "Jack, Marsha, it is a pleasure to meet you: obviously I wish it were under better circumstances, but welcome anyway. First things first: Cell phones please, and by the way, our home is yours for as long as you wish to stay."

Bridger smiled. "Thanks, that's very kind of you. Our cell phones are about thirty miles back in a field of mud. Lauren warned us, though I am not so sure her sources regarding cell phones are on the ball."

"Everyone's cell phone has the capacity to be

turned into a microphone by the powers that be. They can listen to your conversation wherever you are." Aaron said.

"Surely that is a little bit of an over the top fable." Jack couldn't hide his disbelief.

"Not at all. I used to work for the NSA, and I can assure you she was understating the case," Aaron smiled. "The ability of the shadow governments of the world to not only listen to you but virtually track your every move is a reality that is fast becoming an old style. New devices, programs and so on are coming on the scene on almost a daily basis. George Orwell and his "1984" are now a very present reality. Take my word for it. I helped design some of their monitoring programs. There is a frantic race between nations to be first in this field.

"The latest cell phones have facial recognition, and the plan behind it all is to soften us up until we become so blind to the almost total loss of our privacy. Once they achieve that goal, we will willingly take what the Bible calls the Mark of the Beast: a system where every man, woman, and child will take some sort of ID on their body with a numbered code that adds to six hundred and sixty-six. No need for credit cards or in some cases, no need for passwords.

The cash machine or supermarket checkout, the computer, cell phone, front door or private area will simply read your face or the implanted ID that is coming and open: no need for Ali Baba and "open sesame."

Aaron continued, warming to his subject, "For instance, the camera on your cell phone and computer can be switched on without you knowing. Some of the guys at the NSA used to connect and watch girls walking naked around their apartments after having a shower or having just undressed for bed. Though, of course, that was totally illegal I have seen some guys do it when they were on a quiet, boring night shift or when they thought no one was watching them. So my advice is close the laptop or cover the camera with tape and pocket the cell phone, so it prevents the Peeping Toms out there in cyberland from letting you give them a free porn show.

"But I am rambling while you guys need to get yourselves cleaned up. Forgive me, but it's my pet subject."

"I must be living in a dream world," Jack pulled a face. "So you are telling me the Matrix is real? We are living in a Surveillance State."

"One that is given over to the powers of Satan, though many involved in the lower levels of technology have no idea of the truly demonic origin of many of the ideas and inventions that are flooding the planet and what the ultimate goal is."

Goldberg led the group into the lounge area. It was a large oblong room with two settees facing each other. Each settee had its own small oak coffee table set in front of it. Behind one settee was a small bookcase containing various Christian study books, DVDs, and a half a dozen Bibles. Behind the other was a window that faced a small garden. A large TV screen hung on one wall at the back of the room.

In one corner of the room sat a huge armchair and in it, curled up with her head resting on one of the arms was Hal's private secretary Lauren.

As Jack thanked his hosts, he glanced around the room and suddenly noticed her.

Her eyes were red and her cheeks wet with weeping. Her face was drawn and pale, giving her the look of someone much older than her thirty-two years.

Jack strode over to her, the anger welling up inside him. "Lauren, what did you mean when we spoke earlier? Who are these people and were you mixed up in the attempted kidnapping of my wife," he demanded.

Aaron stepped between them. "Mister Bridger, Jack, she is pretty messed up, man. Just give her a few moments. Take your shower, get changed and we'll talk."

Hal placed his hand on Jack's elbow and pulled him back toward the hallway. "Jack, he's right. Let's the three of us shower, get changed, then talk."

Jack glared at Lauren and turned away. "Okay, but she'd better know I'll break every bone in her body if I find out she's involved in the kidnapping attempt on Marsha or Harry's death." He turned back to face the tearful girl. "I'll break your neck if you don't tell me everything. D'you hear me?" The girl broke into a fresh flood of tears and heaving sobs as she buried her face into the arm of the chair.

"Okay, my friend," Aaron broke in, stepping between Jack and Lauren. "That's enough. I know you are pretty messed up, yourself, but you will get nowhere like that. Now please, we want to help you in any way we can but at the moment you are in my home and when you are in my home we play by my rules, understand?" Jack, his face almost purple with anger, looked into Goldberg's face, gave a swift nod of his head, then swung around and stormed out of the room, pulling Marsha behind him.

Hal sighed and moved toward the crying heap in the armchair. "Thanks, Aaron," he said as he patted his friend on the shoulder. "He'll be okay. But we are all at the end of our rope. When I've showered, we'll fill you in. We've all had one heck of a day, and that's no exaggeration. Give them a little space. Jack especially is scared and tired. He witnessed a murder, became a believer in the supernatural and almost lost his wife all in one day."

Hal stood by the edge of the coffee table and laid his hand on the weeping girl's head.

"Lauren, what on earth have you gotten into?" She looked up, red-eyed, into his face. "Hal, I am so sorry. I thought I was onto something really hot for the company. I should have told you."

"Yes, you should have." He stroked her hair in a fatherly fashion.

"I just want everything to go away. I wish I had never involved myself in this: please, believe me, I am terrified now I know what these madmen are planning for us all," she sat upright and wiped her face. "Hal, they plan to produce a world leader. They call him "The promised seed" but he's evil: a mega deception the like of which we've never seen before. They don't call him Jesus or Christ, but they use other names."

"What names, Lauren?"

"Hal, they call him The Seed, the Pseudo-Messiah, but I think he is the one you have spoken about to me before at work, and as I said earlier, he may be the Antichrist."

Chapter 12

Marsha showered and dressed first, and then feeling refreshed began to help lay the table for dinner.

After Hal and Jack had finished showering and changed into fresh clothes, they reappeared downstairs where Dinah had prepared strong coffee for them.

Dinner was served at nine in the dining room, and for the first five minutes, the little group sat in almost complete silence around the large marble table.

Finally, Marsha broke the silence.

"So, Dinah, Aaron how long have you known Hal and Stacey?"

Dinah smiled, "My goodness, about ten years, I guess. When we came over here from the States, we met Hal and Stacey at a Christian Conference, and that was it: Yanks bonding together in a new country made us friends ever since." She sighed. "But I never guessed for a moment we'd be involved in what appears to be a clear fulfillment of ancient Bible prophecies."

"Prophecies?" Marsha tilted her head to one side. "What do you mean?"

"We believe what we are experiencing in the Middle East, Europe, and what Lauren has shared with us briefly before you arrived, has a direct bearing on the return of Jesus Christ. But you are tired, and I am sure Hal will be able to fill in all the blank spots concerning the prophecies as we go along."

Aaron nodded in agreement and said, "Before we go down that road, why don't we ask Hal, Jack and Marsha, to tell us their stories from the beginning? Lauren has told us some, but you arrived as she really got started."

For the next forty-five minutes, the three related the events of the previous twenty-four hours, pausing to answer questions, as the others listened intently, barely believing what they were hearing.

Finally, all eyes turned to Lauren. "Take your time," Stacey in her usual motherly fashion, gently put her arm around the girl's shoulders.

Lauren took in a deep breath and scarcely daring to look into their faces, especially Jack's, she began. "About a month and a half ago, maybe two, I was approached by a man in the Lion's Head, y'know, the pub restaurant just off Whitehall?" Hal nodded, Jack Bridger simply glared.

"He said he had heard that I worked for I.N.S.

and he had a story for me if I wanted it. It was the usual You can't miss this story: it's huge spiel. Well, I was offered a cut of any money I.N.S. paid for the so-called scoop, and I was so excited I jumped at the opportunity without thinking."

"And it was a big story?"

Lauren nodded. "Yes, it was big. Biggest story I have ever come across. He even part-paid me in advance of you paying him; he was so sure you would want to air it on Jack's show. He knew no one else would dare."

Hal, who was sitting across from Lauren, leaned forward. "What was this world-shaking story, Lauren?"

"As I told you, Hal, now I tell you all, there is a secret cabal of powerful men around the world who plan to bring to power a man they call Pseudo-Messiah or the Seed. I guess many would call him the Antichrist. From what I have since learned, that is exactly who he will be: the Antichrist. I know how crazy this must all sound, sitting here, safe, comfortable, eating supper together. But believe me what I am telling you is the absolute truth. Your friend who died earlier today also knew this, and that is why they killed him and will take out anyone who attempts to expose them. I would guess it is that information, and perhaps more, we will find on the flash drive Jack found.

"The cabal meet secretly every few months and have done so since before the outbreak of the Second World War, passing on their knowledge and plans to those family members and recruits who take over when they are either too old, infirm or simply pass away. But one thing: once you're in, there's no back- door."

Hal nodded, fully understanding what was being shared. "Where do these meetings take place?"

"They meet at various locations, various countries. Kind of like the Bilderberg Group or Bohemian Grove in California: but far more powerful and immensely more dangerous and secretive. It was when I discovered what they do in these meetings and what the ultimate plans for the planet are, that I began to pull away: I became scared.

"I set up a meeting with my contact through a pre-arranged drop-off point in the city. I was going to tell him I was through with it and didn't want to carry on. He never showed, and when I checked the dead letter drop, the message I had left him was still there. I had previously followed him to his home in Bayswater, just to see where he lived, so I went there. A policeman was standing outside, so I casually showed him my press card and asked what the problem was. He said it was a suspected suicide, but asked me to keep it under my hat until they issued a press release. I didn't need to ask anymore. I knew it was him.

"I attended the inquest a few days later, and the final verdict was he had taken his own life by slitting his wrist. They didn't even bother to note that he was left-handed and the cut had been on his left wrist."

Stacey interrupted, "But Lauren that still wouldn't have prevented him from using his right hand to slit his left wrist. Most of those types of suicides tend to go for the left wrist."

"But I am sure he didn't commit suicide."

"I am not saying you are wrong, Lauren, but how can you be so certain."

"My contact's name was Jeff Michelson. You know the name?"

"Yes, I know the name," Hal replied. "Never met the guy, though. I understand he sometimes rang the office with some interesting little scandal or other in the hope we would pay him for the use of it. But I still don't know how you can be so sure he didn't commit suicide."

"I am sure, boss. I am sure because when Jeff

was in the Special Forces in Iraq, he was shot up badly and invalided out of the service," She paused. "Boss, Jeff Michelson was disabled. He could barely use his right arm to wipe his nose, let alone stick a knife into his left wrist and draw blood. He had the minimalist bit of feeling in his right arm."

"My Lord. You mean they killed him?"

"Yes, and these people are so influential and powerful they were able to cover it up. But now they are after every one of us in this room.

"Their resources are global and terrifyingly efficient: satellite, GPS tracking, web cameras, CCTV, hidden microphones. They are gradually gaining control of them all." She paused again and shivered. "They are even able to utilize your TV or computer to watch what you are doing, open your cell phones to locate you and listen to you and so much more. You must be so careful who you take into your confidence, boss. They are adept at dropping their people into relationships with the targets they are watching.

"They fooled Jeff so completely for a while. He really believed they were a bunch of high ranking do-gooders. They use all kinds of methods to convince you what they are doing is for the greater good. But just like Hal said regarding Harry Langston, once Jeff discovered what they are planning he backed off and that's when he wanted to expose them, and so he contacted me. I don't know why he didn't call the office as he always did with other news stories he came up with. Guess Jeff was so scared they would be listening in on his cell phone. He told me he had watched where I went for lunch and just waited there for me one day and introduced himself. Also, they use other, more unconventional, methods."

"What do you mean unconventional methods?" asked Hal, although he knew exactly what she meant.

"You will not believe me, but they use some kind of supernatural power." She waited for everyone to laugh at the very suggestion but no one moved. Hal and Jack exchanged glances.

"We believe you," they said in unison, but Lauren didn't seem to catch on to their meaning.

"So I guess we have you to thank for today. It was you who told them about my meeting with Harry Langston wasn't it," Jack Bridger said, his eyes narrowing as his anger began to rise again.

"I told them, yes. It was Jeff who told me they have some sort of link to the supernatural. That sounds crazy, right? But I believe it."

Jack looked around the table, then back at Lauren.

"Yes, Lauren. Twenty-four hours ago I would have said you are crazy: completely off your rocker. But after today, and the two out of this world encounters I have had, my whole belief system has taken a major shift. I don't think you are crazy. You are just a damned greedy, stupid little idiot for getting yourself and the rest of us into what could easily cost us our lives. Whatever possessed you, girl? Why didn't you warn us off earlier?"

"I am sorry," she blurted. "That's all I can say. I am so very sorry." Her eyes filled again, and she hung her head. "All I saw was a scoop for I.N.S. and some kudos around the office. Stupid and greedy, I agree.

"Anyway, a few days later, after the inquest, I started getting anonymous, untraceable calls. Threatening me, warning me I could go to jail, or worse, I could follow my dead friend if I didn't keep my mouth shut and do exactly as they demanded. I realized they had been watching Jeff and me all along. Jeff had told me Mister Langston had specific dangerous information and now these guys were ordering me, with threats, to let them know immediately if I picked up any information or if there was any contact between him and I.N.S.. They knew he was a friend of Hal so naturally I was in a prime position to keep them informed. Because I listened in on private calls, I knew Hal was in touch with Mister Langston, and Hal always used a secure line when speaking with private individuals. So presumably they were unable to listen in to all of Hal and Langston's conversations. I let them know every time Hal and Langston called each other.

"I figured they didn't dare kill Langston because they didn't know what he had done with the evidence he had gotten a hold of. They were happy to listen in on his calls whenever they were able and have me confirm any decisions made by Hal after he finished the call. How wrong was I?" She gazed down at the table.

"Ultimately, I knew I was on borrowed time when I overheard Hal and Mister Langston set up the meeting with Jack. I stood outside your office door, Hal and heard everything. So I let them know.

"I was so scared. I just wanted out, so I left a message at a pre-arranged place on my way home that night, hoping to God this would be the end of it all and my part in it would not come to light."

"What on earth were you thinking?" Stacey placed her hand over her mouth as she spoke.

"I thought, I hoped, Jack would get the info, Mister Langston would go into hiding and somehow they would both outwit these men and Hal would publish whatever revelations were gained from Langston. But deep down I knew there was no escaping these people."

"So, initially, you got greedy," Jack spat through his teeth.

"Yes, alright, I have already told you I got greedy," she replied without looking up.

"And as a result of your greed Harry Langston is dead, my wife was almost kidnapped and we are now in danger of losing our lives," Bridger slammed his fist on the table. "You stupid, irresponsible little fool. Do you have any idea what you have done? We are now fighting some unimaginable force of combined elitist and evil otherworldly powers. Why didn't you tell us? You should have let us help you."

Lauren hung her head and said nothing.

There was a long silence and everyone around the table was again aware of the immensity of the war they had fallen into.

Hal broke the silence. "Well, now we have an idea of what we are up against it is no use placing blame and shouting. This is where we are and our next move must be to see what is on the flash drive. It's time we took a look."

Chapter 13

Aaron pushed his chair away from the table.

"Okay, folks. Hal is right; we must move fast and try to keep one step ahead of them. Jack, you have the flash drive?"

Jack stood up, his eyes still boring into Lauren's downturned head.

"Yeah, I have it. I took it from my filthy shirt when I took a shower. Here." He removed the drive from his trouser pocket and handed it to Goldberg.

The little group of seven went to Aaron's office at the back of the house and crowded into the room.

It was large with what appeared to be old manuscripts piled on the top of shelves filled with books lining the walls.

In one corner sat a collection of technical hardware that for a moment caused Marsha to draw in her breath.

"Wow, what have you got here?"

"Toys for boys, my friend." Aaron sat at his desk and turned on the computer. A forty inch wall screen sprang to life and he inserted the flash drive into a socket.

The group pressed closer to see what would appear but were stunned to see a mass of numbers crisscrossing the screen.

"It's encrypted," Jack Bridger cursed.

"As expected," Goldberg chuckled. "But, we shall see what we shall see." He pressed a few keys and a new page appeared.

Dinah said "This is Aaron's playpen. I heard him tell you, Jack, he used to work in for the NSA in the States. He worked on encryption, but when he left the department, he brought his brain with him," she ruffled her hand through his hair and kissed him on the back of his head. "What you and I regard as impossible, my husband eats for breakfast."

"Well, don't speak too soon, my love," said Aaron. "I haven't used those skills for some time. But let's see." He screwed up his eyes. "If I try this." For the next few minutes, his fingers played the keyboard like a concert pianist. As he did so a new set of figures finally appeared and began running through various computations.

"Hopefully, that will do it eventually." He stood up and looked around at everyone.

"What do you mean, eventually?" Marsha asked. "We need this info. asap."

"And you will get it asap. Surely you didn't expect to open this up and have everything fall into our laps at the press of a key? From what

Lauren, Jack and Hal have told us, the people we are up against are obviously very powerful and the information so important in no way would Langston put their plans on a USB for all to read. This will have been buried, encrypted beneath several layers and I am sure there will be at least two passwords to get into the real meat."

"So what do we do in the meantime?"

Dinah turned to Stacey. "We pray." They nodded in unison.

"Pray?" asked Lauren. "You can't be serious." Stacey replied, "You have already agreed these people use supernatural forces to promote at least part of their plans for us all. So why shouldn't we do likewise in our fight against them? Only, we shall go one better and engage with God himself rather than the fallen demonic spirits they contact. That is not to say our fight will be without serious risks to ourselves, but believe me, to ask the aid of God and the angels is an absolute essential as we go into whatever lies ahead. Not to do so would be the greatest madness imaginable."

They piled back into the lounge as Dinah and Stacey exited to the dining room and the kitchen to clear away the remains of the evening meal. Marsha and Jack attempted to follow them but were stopped by Dinah.

"My dear new friends, after what you have been through today, you expect to slave in the kitchen?"

"Believe me, we need to do something normal after today's excitement," Marsha said as she and Jack picked up some plates and prepared them for the dishwasher.

"I thought you said *pray*?" Lauren asked as she joined the women and began tidying.

"Definitely," said Dinah. "But I am still human and I know the moment I begin to pray my mind will fill with thoughts about the washing up, taking my focus off really important matters."

"She's right," added Stacey. "I know so many people who get down to pray in church on a Sunday and the moment they do they get the thought *Did I leave the cooker on*? It's old, but a very effective ploy of Satan."

Lauren closed her eyes and shook her head in bewilderment. "Well, I don't know anything about praying. Haven't done anything like that since Sunday School."

"Me neither," said Marsha. In fact, I didn't even get to Sunday School. My folks are complete atheists and I was brought up the same way. Though I'd say, I am more agnostic.

Just not sure if there is a God out there watching us. I'd like to think there is some nice old guy in the sky looking out for me. So unlike Lauren and you guys, prayer is a completely foreign language to me."

"Well, now is the time to open the hotline to heaven, ladies." Stacey made the comment sound more like an order.

Dinah, Marsha, and Stacey collected the remnants, cleaned the plates and utensils and Jack put them in the dishwasher. Lauren wasn't sure what to do so retreated to her armchair.

Once everyone was back in the lounge and seated Aaron took the lead, his dark eyes shining as he looked around the room.

"Okay, everyone. This is how I see it. Lauren, Hal, Jack, and Marsha have experienced a situation that far exceeds anything they envisaged just twenty-four hours ago. It has now resulted in the murder in broad daylight of Harry Langston and the attempted kidnapping of Jack's wife."

"Call me Marsha."

"Okay, Marsha," He grinned.

Jack shot a look at Lauren but she avoided his gaze and looked dead ahead at Aaron. She knew he was looking at her. She could feel his eyes burning into her and the anger he felt for her at that moment. A lump formed in her throat and she wanted to burst into tears again, but she swallowed hard and intensified her concentration on what was being said.

Lauren Hutton wasn't generally given to tears. Having been brought up on the wrong side of the tracks in the East end of London, she had grown up with three brothers, a permanently drunken mother, and an almost continually absent father who spent more time in Her Majesty's Pleasure than he did with his family.

At twelve years old, she had seen her eldest brother gunned down in a gang battle in the middle of the street and had cradled his head in her lap as he slipped into eternity. She cried then. But somehow the tears had dried and she had never cried since. Not until today when she realized she had betrayed the only family she had come to know and love: Hal and Stacey, Jack and Marsha.

No, she had not cried again until today, not even when her mother used to beat her in a drunken rage. Lauren had decided then and there to get out of the dead-end life she was living.

Her two remaining brothers left home almost at the same time and joined the army, both rising in the ranks and loving military life.

Meanwhile, Lauren knuckled down and forced herself to become a model student, cutting herself off from the gang she had run with since the age of ten. She made new friends and eventually made the grade good enough for University.

The last words she heard her mother shout as she packed to leave were "What the hell do you think you'll become, smart girl?" Then she had laughed. A cackling laugh made all the more effective through years of heavy drinking and smoking. "You're a nothing! D'ya hear? A nothing: have always been and always will be.

"You're just a useless no-hoper who thinks she's someone because she can answer stupid questions on an exam paper. Well, off you go, genius. But I'll see you again in a few weeks when you wake up and see you belong here and not with those snotty-nosed know-it-alls. You'll be back." She cackled again and sucked in a long drag of a cigarette.

Lauren closed the front door behind her and never saw her mother again.

She graduated with honors in journalism and then went on to do some secretarial work. After working her way up the pay scale writing for various magazines and some freelancing, she jumped at the chance to join the I.N.S. working for Hal and Stacey. Now she felt her whole world had caved in because of her greed and stupidity. She had betrayed the very people that had become more family to her than her own dysfunctional ties.

She was close to tears again. But she resolved "no tears, now." She wanted to help put right the mess she had helped create. She tuned back into Aaron when she heard him mentioned her name.

"Lauren has also now become the target of these shady, powerful people due to her involvement with her contact who we must accept was also murdered. And once they wake up to the fact she has fallen off the radar, they will easily guess she is with us and has told us all she knows. They will be even more determined to repay her for her opening her mouth." Lauren shuddered.

Aaron continued, "If that were not enough, we are up against an even more powerful enemy that is not human. We have stepped into a deadly battle, a battle against the powers of darkness."

He glanced around the room at his friends. "I have to say I believe before this is over, some, or all of us could forfeit our lives for whatever is contained on that flash drive in my office, or as a result of what we decide to do with that information.

"I am afraid the forces ranged against us are determined to see to it that whatever is hidden on it remains hidden. To keep it that way they will not stop until it is back in their possession and we are all six feet under. We are most certainly marked for death. No matter if we were to tell them we have no idea what the item contains, they will kill us just to be sure."

Hal nodded, "That's right, Aaron, just as I told Jack. These people will not stop in their search for us. Let's pray, right now. The coming days and weeks will find us pitted against a formidable enemy. One that has all the forces of evil on its side. We desperately need to be guided and helped by God and His Holy Spirit." He lowered his head and closed his eyes. The others followed, including Jack, Marsha, and Lauren, who, though they were not used to calling on heaven for help, agreed there was no avenue on earth from where they could get the help and protection they now needed so desperately.

"Father," Hal began. "We are now in such need of your guidance and help. You know what and who it is we are up against and how those who hate us want our lives snuffed out. But we thank you, oh, Lord, you are the helper of the helpless and the protection of those who fear you. Please, Lord, show us how to use the information we now have and at the same time show us the way forward. Give us wisdom, strength, guidance and protection in these days. In Jesus' name, we pray. Amen."

Chapter 14

As the little group sat in silence, they gradually became aware of a sense of peace gently enveloping them and replacing the previous tension they had all felt.

First Hal slipped to his knees, then Stacey, Aaron and Dinah followed one after the other as an almost tangible physical presence filled the room.

Dinah whispered, "Yeshua, Lord Jesus, we..." she stopped as the little group was engulfed by a sense of incredible love.

Jack, Marsha, and Lauren remained sitting, feeling embarrassed and not knowing what to do. None of them had been in a church for years apart from weddings and funerals. A prayer meeting was something completely alien to them. Yet the sense of someone else, someone unseen, in the room was overwhelming. The overpowering awareness of love and acceptance that now surrounded them brought their deepest emotions to the surface.

In the silence, Jack was surprised to feel tears forming in his eyes and a real desire in his heart to thank God for rescuing him and Marsha earlier in the day. He spoke softly,

"Jesus, I don't know what to say apart from thank you for saving my life today and for helping us rescue Marsha. I am so in need of you at this moment. I don't know how, but I want to be a follower of yours, please. I know how many bad things I have done in my life and the crazy unbelief I have harbored when it came to believing in you. But today, today I just know you are real. I am more certain of that than anything I have ever believed in.

"Today, I know it was you who spoke to me, who helped me escape certain death and who saw to it Hal and I were able to rescue Marsha. I don't know how I know all this, but I know it," he felt a lump forming in his throat. "I know you are real, Jesus and I am so sorry for ever doubting your existence. Please forgive me."

He slipped to his knees and burying his face into the seat of the chair he let the tears come in a torrent of previously pent-up emotion.

As he did, a sure knowledge that his prayer had been heard flooded his being, so much so that through his tears he began to laugh quietly. Hal looked over at him. "You okay?" he asked. Jack looked up, tears dripping from his chin but his face almost radiant. "Hal, I am fine. I feel so, so free and clean. I don't know why, can't explain what's happening to me, but I know things will turn out okay." He felt an arm slide around his shoulders and turned to see Marsha with tears streaming down her face as she slipped off the settee and knelt beside her husband. She closed her eyes and rested her head on Jack's shoulder.

"Jesus, I am not a praying person. Don't know how," she began. "But I want to thank you for looking after my husband and me today. I don't understand this at all, but if you really are there, please forgive me too and help me to follow you. And please show us the next move we should make and please protect us all...um," she felt her face flush with shyness. "Amen, I guess."

Hal moved around and knelt beside Jack, while Stacey sat on the settee stroking Marsha's hair and holding her hand.

The room fell silent as they drank in the awesome sense of God's presence.

They rested in the silence for another fifteen minutes. Finally, Aaron spoke. "Thank you, Lord, for saving souls. Thank you for Jack our new brother in the faith and thank you for dear Marsha our new sister in the Messiah. Bless them both and keep these new children of yours safe. May they be strong in the Lord God of Israel doing exploits for you in these end days. Please use us to get the information out and awake everyone to what is happening, whatever the cost to ourselves."

After a few more minutes of silence, no one wanting to break the incredible peace in the room, they gradually stood up and looked at each other.

Jack and Lauren locked eyes. She stood, still not fully understanding what had just taken place.

He felt the same old anger begin to rise, then unbelievably, it disappeared "I...I have no idea why I am doing this," Jack stammered. "But come here." He wrapped his arms around Lauren's body and hugged her as her arms fell limp at her side in shock and disbelief. "But I have hurt you so much," she said. "I have let all of you down: your friend murdered, almost got Marsha kidnapped, the rest of us literally on the run from the Devil himself. I am so sorry. I can't say it enough. I am so sorry, everyone."

This time she did break and once again gave way to tears, burying her face into Jack's chest and putting her arms around him.

The others gathered around in a group hug.

"What's done is done," Dinah said, patting the sobbing girl's back. "Now we are a team.

Looking out for each other."

Aaron added, "That, and with God's help, is the only way we are going to come through this alive."

Jack Bridger gently pushed Lauren out at arm's length. "Yes, we are in this together, together, yeah?" Lauren wiped her eyes and nodded. "Thank you, Jack. Thanks, everyone. I am so..." "Sorry," they all said smiling at her. She nodded again and smiled.

"Yeah, well, just so as you know."

"We do, Lauren, and we forgive," Hal said, looking at Jack, who nodded.

Dinah broke in. "It's late, dear ones. I don't know about you newsy guys who stay up 'til all hours, but I am shattered and need my bed."

"That's my practical wife speaking," laughed Goldberg. "Yes, we should all get some shut eye."

"You are right," said Hal. "Let's get to bed and get some needed rest. Something tells me in the days ahead; we may not be getting the chance of a good night's sleep as easily as we have been used to in the past."

They all agreed and bidding one another good night; they ascended the stairs to the bedrooms.

Jack and Marsha undressed and almost fell into bed. They were both emotionally and physically exhausted. After exchanging thoughts on the day's events, they finally kissed and fell asleep in each other's arms.

Holding each other in the darkness, somehow they knew whatever lay ahead, they were now loved and safe in the family of God.

Lauren undressed and slipped into bed. It had been the most unusual day of her life. She lay in the darkness, wondering. "*Is God real? Did he really rescue Jack and Marsha and Hal today? What about that prayer meeting?*" She smiled to herself. "*That was bizarre, and yet incredible. Someone wonderful was in that room with us. I just know it. I wonder if the others felt it too. I really do love these people...and ...*" The words came so easily. "I really do love you, Jesus." She said out loud as she slid out of bed and knelt down.

"Jesus," she whispered. "I really do love you. Thank you for all you have done. Hal always told me you died on the cross for my sins. I have fought tooth and nail against giving my life over to you. I was so wrong. I believe it, I really do believe you died for me and although I can't explain it, I believe you were somehow there with us tonight." The very thought sent shivers of excitement through her body and she quietly exclaimed "Wow, oh, wow! Jesus, would you please do for me what you have done for the others? Please forgive me and make me yours forever. I have never been so sure of anything than right now wanting to know you, please. Amen" She climbed back into bed and fell into the sweetest sleep she had ever known.

Chapter 15

The next morning the little band of believers met around the breakfast table in the kitchen and discussed what their next plan of action should be.

Aaron sipped his coffee and said, "Well, until the flash drive coughs up whatever it is hiding there is little we can do, is there?"

Hal agreed, "No, that is true, but I think in the meantime, it would be of benefit to us all to all be up to par in our understanding, as best as we can, of what and who we are up against."

Jack replied. "Marsha and I are both complete novices in any of this spiritual chicanery you say we are facing, Hal. So I am all for being more informed if it helps us get to wherever this is leading."

"Me, too," Lauren chimed in. "But before we start can I just say something?"

"You aren't going to say sorry again are you?" Dinah joked and squeezed Lauren's hand.

Lauren laughed out loud for the first time then blushed. "No. I think you all know how crushed I was for letting you all down," she stammered. "I just want you to know how much I love you all and to tell you last night I spoke to God," her face reddened.

"I gave my life to him and became a Christian."

The kitchen suddenly reverberated with cheering. Hal walked around the table and gave Laren such a hug he almost crushed her ribs.

After the excitement of Lauren's testimony, Hal said "Right, so everyone in this room is now a believer in the Lord Jesus Christ. Yesterday there were four of us believers and now we are seven. That is absolutely awesome. And that also means we are, individually and as a group, in Satan's crosshairs. And that makes it all the more imperative we are, to use a well-worn phrase, reading from the same page. I suggest we have breakfast, then move into the lounge."

"Agreed," said Dinah as she laid out the breakfast cutlery, bowls, milk, and cereals.

"And toast is on the way courtesy of our chef for today, Aaron Goldberg."

They all laughed as Aaron bowed and produced slices of toast in the rack.

They chatted freely over the next forty minutes as they ate, drank coffee and relived the previous day's events, and then they retired to the lounge.

"Over to you, Hal," smiled Aaron, as everyone

made themselves comfortable. Lauren felt so at home she sat on the carpet with her back to Marsha's chair while Marsha rested her hand on her shoulder. Hal said, "I don't know quite where to begin so please stay with me here because I am going way back in time.

"I guess we have all heard of Adam and Eve, Satan, the serpent, in the garden and so on. And how sin entered the human race through Adam and Eve's disobedience against God when they listened to Satan's lies. God promised through Eve and her descendants the Messiah would come. He would be known as the Seed of the woman. Aaron, may I have your Bible for a moment, please?"

Hal leafed through the opening chapters of the book of Genesis until he came to chapter three and verse fifteen. He cleared his throat and read: *And I will put enmity between thee and the woman, and between thy seed and her seed; it shall bruise thy head, and thou shalt bruise his heel.*

Hal closed the book and continued. "In this verse, there is the promise of a coming Messiah who would crush Satan. Jesus is that promised seed of the woman. But who is the seed of Satan the serpent? We believe that to be a reference to the coming Antichrist. He is also known to many in the Black Arts as the Seed of the Beast. So Antichrist, the seed of Satan, will be at war against Yeshua, the real Hebrew name for Jesus, the seed of the woman. This also can be seen as a prophecy of a battle between God and Satan for the souls of men and women. A battle that will carry on throughout history and culminate in the physical appearance of Satan's seed: the Antichrist, in the final days of earth's history before Yeshua returns from heaven and defeats Antichrist at the Battle of Armageddon."

"But let me get this straight," Dinah cut in.

"Are you saying Antichrist will be born supernaturally just like Jesus?"

Hal smiled. "Not quite. To use a double negative, Satan cannot create life from nothing. He isn't God. He is a rebellious fallen angel. Jesus was born without the normal man-woman relationship. His birth was totally unique. God planted the seed, that is Jesus, in Mary's womb while she was still a virgin." He drew in his breath. "However, it is believed if the seed of the woman, the Messiah, was born miraculously yet as a physical human being, and then at his baptism he was filled with the Holy Spirit, so too will the Antichrist be born as a physical human being but by some deviant satanic sex act with Satan. Through a woman, a willing carrier, if you will, who will birth Satan's seed. Then at some later date, he will undergo a parody of Christ's baptism by being taken over by a demonic spirit."

Dinah interrupted. "But, Hal didn't Yeshua say angels cannot have sex and procreate?"

"No, he didn't. He said the believers in heaven will be as the angels and not marry. Angels do not marry or procreate even though it may appear from scripture that they are able to for some reason because it says the ones who rebelled in Genesis six did just that: impregnating human women and from those encounters men of great stature were born."

Hal read from Genesis chapter six.

And it came to pass, when men began to multiply on the face of the earth, and daughters were born unto them, That the sons of God saw the daughters of men that they were fair; and they took them wives of all which they chose.

And the Lord said, My spirit shall not always strive with man, for that he also is flesh: yet his days shall be an hundred and twenty years.

There were giants in the earth in those days; and also after that, when the sons of God came in unto the daughters of men, and they bare children to them, the same became mighty men which were of old, men of renown.

Hal closed the Bible. "There is the belief among many Christians and Jews that the term sons of God, refers to the descendants of Adam's son Seth. That belief only came about in the fourth century. Before that, both Jews and Christians alike believed this scripture was talking about the sexual encounters of human women with fallen angels. There seems to be no logical reason why the descendants of Seth would father children that become mighty men or giants. But if we go with the belief of the early Church and the ancient Jewish Rabbis who believed this referred to fallen angels interacting with women it makes complete sense.

"Wow! I have never heard any of this," exclaimed Dinah.

Hal pressed on. "Okay, so there was a connection between this earth and fallen angels from another realm or another dimension. It was common knowledge among many of the ancient civilizations that the giant monoliths seen dotted about the earth were the remains of building projects undertaken by these giants. The Great Pyramid of Giza, Egypt, for instance, or pyramids found around the planet, defy our modern architects as to how they were built. In Ecuador, a pyramid eighty meters or almost one hundred yards in height has been discovered with stones each weighing over two tonnes.

"There are many such structures around the planet. But the legends that have come down to us from those times agree: they were built by or under the guidance of, the gods who came down from the skies. Many researchers believe these buildings are the result of interaction with fallen angels and their giant offspring.

"Modern technology cannot match the skill and perfection of these monoliths. You cannot slide a paper between the blocks; they are placed together so precisely.

"But the giants died out and the gods returned to the skies promising to return one day. In India, the legends of the gods being able to fly through the sky in craft named virahnas in many ways mirror our modern day reports of UFO's, unidentified flying objects. Many mock the idea of such things, but when they are reported by competent military personnel and not merely Joe Blow after a night on the town, they become more real than just being passed off as the results of last night's drinking session. Many researchers believe the ones who pilot the UFO's are the same beings that fathered the giants and flew virahnas in ancient times. In case you think I am going off track here just hold on with me a little longer.

Chapter 16

Hal sipped his coffee. "So, let's come up to more modern times. The Second World War.

"Ever heard of Foo fighters?"

"The pop group?"

"No," Hal's mouth forced a smile. "Foo fighters was the name given by both allied and enemy pilots during the Second World War. They appeared as small globes of light, apparently intelligently piloted. They buzzed planes from both sides, German and allied, flying at incredible speeds and vanishing as fast as they had appeared. No one ever discovered what they were, who or what piloted them or where they came from. To this day they remain a mystery. But the same phenomenon had shown up elsewhere long before the Second World War."

"When?"

"In Nineteen seventeen, for instance, in Fatima, Portugal. Three children witnessed the apparent visitation of a being claiming to be the Virgin Mary in a small cove, the Cova de Iria, as they were tending sheep from their small village. During several subsequent visitations, the same small globes of light appeared flying around the area. In fact, the lady first appeared floating in a globe of light.

"Finally, during her final visit, seventy thousand people gathered in the hope of seeing this apparition as no one but the children had seen her. Instead, as the children spoke to the invisible entity claiming to be Mary, the mother of Jesus, the crowd were treated to a dazzling aerial display by what we today would call a UFO.

"It had been raining heavily and everyone was soaked to the skin. Suddenly a disc came through the parting clouds, spinning and shooting out bright multi-colored rays of light.

"The object fell toward the earth, the heat from it drying the ground and the people's clothing as it did so. It then shot back into the heavens.

" Most of the very religious witnesses believed the sun had been dislodged from the heavens and had begun to fall to earth. They believed God had sent them a sign from heaven confirming the visions witnessed by the three children. But of course, it wasn't the sun.

"Observatories around the world recorded no such event. The sun never moved out of position at all." Hal paused and took in a deep breath.

"Mass hallucination, maybe," Lauren said.

"Afraid not," Hal continued. "People as far away as nine miles from the event witnessed the object descending and receding into the clouds.

"The series of visions and the mysterious messages the lady subsequently gave to the children has become known as the Three Secrets of Fatima. The first two were made public, but the final secret was said to contain warnings of an apocalypse so terrible the church has never released it, even though the Vatican did release what they claimed was the final secret, hand-written by one of the children. It was later discovered the handwriting was not the same as that on the original. Also, the original was written on one sheet of paper while the one released by the Vatican was written on four."

Jack scratched his head. "They are holding it back."

"Exactly" Hal agreed. "But why, no one knows. We can only speculate as to the contents of the final message. Maybe we'll never know for sure.

"Let me move on and I'll show the connection in a moment. Let's come to events just after the war. Have any of you ever heard of Project Paper Clip?"

"Some kind of conspiracy theory about ex-Nazis coming to America, wasn't it? I think someone told me about it a long time ago, but I dismissed it at once as nonsense," Marsha replied.

"No, it isn't nonsense," Hal frowned. "What I am going to share with you is common knowledge in many quarters, especially among those in high government positions and the intelligence community, and for the most part, it can be documented.

"It comes as a huge shock to many to discover our governments have been hoodwinking us for decades, possibly much longer if we dare to dig deeper. For us, we must go back to the period just before the end of World War Two, and Project Paperclip," Hal sipped his coffee.

"As the war came to a close, many allied agents in the field were uncovering evidence of the Nazi regime's incredible technological advances.

"These Wunderwaffen or miracle weapons, as the Nazis called them, were so far advanced of the allies there was only one course of action open to the advancing allied armies.

"As it became clear to everyone, apart from Hitler himself, Germany was going to lose the war, America went into overdrive in an effort to get their hands on the best of the best Nazis in the field of rocket science, Physics, germ warfare, engineering, medicine and so on.

"Originally the project was named Operation Overcast and was later changed to Paperclip. The plan was to round up more than three thousand Nazi scientists, secretly get them to America, and debrief them. But once the authorities began to uncover the overwhelming amount of knowledge these men possessed it became obvious they couldn't let them go home. Even today some of the information they possessed is classified. Not that the majority wanted to return to Germany. Many knew they stood a pretty hot chance of being hunted down and tried as war criminals for their activities during the war.

"For instance, the man we call the father of rocket science, Werner Von Braun, was, in fact, the man in charge of building the V1 and V2 rockets that caused so much death and destruction in England, France, and Belgium.

"Would it shock you to know this member of the Nazi party and a member of the dreaded SS, invented the Saturn V rocket that took Neil Armstrong, Buzz Aldrin and Michael Collins to the moon? He would almost certainly have faced charges had he returned to Germany for the role he played, seeing as how thousands of slave laborers worked on his projects.

"Many Nazis had their details changed, without the knowledge and approval of the State Department. Later, many became American citizens. Had the truth been revealed publicly it would have caused a massive scandal, maybe the collapse of the government. At the very least these men would have been viewed as significant security risks.

"These Nazi scientists and engineers were rounded up and shipped to the USA along with their family members. Of course, not all remained in the USA and many found havens elsewhere in countries such as Spain and Argentina with the help of the Catholic Church through what became known as the Vatican Ratlines."

Lauren shook her head, "Woah, I can't see what any of this has to do with what is happening to us here and now. You're talking about events that took place decades ago. But most of those guys who stayed in the USA are long dead and forgotten and I guess most if not all their children have grown up as good Americans and tried to forget and distance themselves from their family's Nazi past."

Jack nodded in agreement, "I agree with

Lauren, what has this to do with what is going on with us? I am lost. I don't know where you are going with this, Hal."

Hal smiled and leaned back in the chair.

"What I am saying is these otherworldly beings have passed themselves off as tender-hearted space aliens who have our best interests at heart. They want to deceive us into believing they are our alien brothers observing us, their wayward siblings here on earth, and are intending to step in when the planned opportunity arises in order to prevent us committing the ultimate madness: the nuclear destruction of all life on the planet and at the same time bring out the Antichrist.

"Their true object is to deceive us all and have us worship their master, Satan himself, through the appearance of the supposed savior of the planet, the Antichrist, the son of the Devil."

Dinah pouted her lips, "This is all very interesting, dear Hal, but I still do not understand what this has to do with our current situation."

"Okay, the monoliths; the Fatima visions; the so-called Foo Fighters of the Second World War; the UFO phenomenon and even our moral and spiritual decline are all linked to what is happening today for one simple reason," he paused and took in a deep breath. "The demonic realm is the guiding hand behind all these events and more whether we believe it or not; it is a fact."

"Oh, come on. Really?" Jack was beginning to think Hal had lost his mind.

"Yes, really. When the Nazi scientists were interrogated following their capture and subsequent entry into the USA, the interrogators suddenly became aware one of the men they had netted held vital information that had been seen by very few apart from Hitler and his inner circle.

"This one man, General Dietrich von Hattendorf, had been given the task of coordinating a plan to bring in a world ruler following the death of the Fuhrer, Hitler or whoever held the reins in the years to come. Of course, the plan was not expected to be implemented for many years, but upon Germany losing the war and the *supposed* suicide of Hitler and his new bride Eva Braun, the plan took on an even greater urgency.

"The Nazis knew they could not continue with the same policies of extermination and ruthless conquest as they had done during the glory days of the Third Reich. The world had to be molded over a long period before it would finally accept a new Reich. So a plan was hatched to prepare the world for the coming ruler. It would take years to bring to fruition, decades in fact. People's minds had to be gradually swayed toward a new Reich, a new Order. But the man who would lead it would be a new Hitler. Oh, not a clone of Hitler. People would never accept that kind of open deception."

Bridger sat on the edge of his chair, "So, what did they do?"

Hal took a few more leisurely few sips of his coffee. "The papers found in General von Hattendorff's possession, which, by the way, he happily exchanged for a new life, new identity and a payoff that would see him settled for the rest of his life, shocked the few people who read them. The plan, my friends, was to work hand in hand with the Vatican as well as the beings who piloted the Foo Fighters or UFOs, to birth a new order in the coming years. An order that would eliminate war because the whole world would come under global governance and the dominance of a Superman: a man inhabited and guided by an alien being.

"I know what I am saying sounds like the

ravings of a top-notch conspiracy lunatic, but I have read the von Hattendorff papers. In them, there is a report detailing Hitler's meeting with a being from one of these craft."

"But why couldn't these beings simply pop down in a UFO and scare us all to death with threats of annihilation if we didn't go along with them?" Jack queried.

"This is real life, not the movie *Earth versus the Flying Saucers*," Hal replied. "Don't you see if they had done as you suggest they could have had a global rebellion on their hands and that is not what they want. They want to deceive us into believing they are benevolent beings with only our best interests at heart."

"When what they really want is....?"

"What they really want is total control and to ultimately take us to the place the Bible calls the Lake of Fire. They are destined to be consigned there by God after Christ returns.

"Their only joy is to deceive God's creation into following them over the cliff edge into the jaws of the Lake of Fire itself."

"But how is that possible if these beings are aliens from some other planet from out in the way beyond?" Marsha was confused.

"Because, as I have just explained, they are not from another planet. They are beings from another dimension. A spiritual dimension inhabited by creatures we call fallen angels. Those same beings we read of in the book of Genesis who procreated with human women. Beings under the leadership of Satan himself, whose only goal is to deceive mankind into believing the same spirit that inhabited all the spiritual greats of the past has returned and now lives within the chosen one: the new Messiah. But he will be one selected by Satan and the global elite to head the World Government.

"In doing so, they intend to establish a regime of global peace: A false Messianic age that will include Christians, Muslims, Jews and just about every other belief on the planet. A melting pot of faiths based in Jerusalem, Rome and the rebuilt city of Babylon, Iraq.

"This false spirituality will accept everyone, uniting the planet. Everyone that is, apart from those who hold to the belief that Jesus Christ is the only way to God."

"But how will they achieve this?"

"By slowly uniting the world, implanting their ideas into the minds of the young especially, through social media.

"In reality, by this seemingly innocent invention, virtually everyone on the planet can be monitored and their thinking gradually directed down the anti-God, anti-Bible path the elite want them to travel.

"And it doesn't stop there. After nine eleven, the government set up the Department of Homeland Security. It may shock you guys to know, the man they called in to do the job was Marcus Wolf. Marcus Wolf was paid millions to create the Department of Homeland Security. He was known as the man with no face. He earned that moniker because Herr Marcus Wolf was the former chief of the East German Secret Police: the Stasi. There's even more. The man they chose to work alongside him was General Yevgeny Primakov the former deputy head of the KGB who later became head of Russia's Foreign Intelligence."

"That's almost unbelievable, Hal," Marsha said.

"It is," Hal replied. "So is it any wonder many researchers call the destruction of the Twin Towers an inside job and the American version of the Reichstag Fire when Hitler's cronies set fire to Germany's Parliament building. Of course, we all know out of that came the German police State.

"I am not suggesting that the entire government of the United States was involved in the destruction of the Twin towers. Or that the two guys brought in to create the Homeland Security system were aware of the shadow government's real intentions.

"But many believe the powers behind the scenes orchestrated those events to bring in more laws that restrict people's freedom.

"The more I research and pray over these and other events, the more I believe the USA especially is begging God for judgment," Hal continued. "Godly men have had visions of America being destroyed by missiles in a war of unprecedented destruction. I believe we are on the verge of seeing just such a judgment fall on America. God may even use Russia or even North Korea to do it. Remember, he used a pagan king, Nebuchadnezzar of Babylon to bring judgment on Israel. He can do it again, only this time it will be a judgment on America.

"Billy Graham once famously said: "If God doesn't judge America, he will have to apologize to Sodom and Gomorrah."

"The elite are not stupid when it comes to spiritual matters, even though they blindly follow the dark path of Lucifer, believing he will win the final battle.

"They plan on creating a major crisis out of

which their man, the Antichrist, will take the reins of global governance in the name of peace and security. It will be a world in total rebellion against God. They may even use a war as the crisis to bring in this global government with the help of the demonic forces behind the scenes as Harry suggested.

"It may be God will allow this, but only as far as furthers his plan for the end times and the return of Yeshua.

"Beside the Antichrist will be a spiritual leader who will sway the masses into accepting and worshipping the new Messiah figure. It will be a global spirituality based on the worship of the new world emperor and the alien - demonic beings that produced him.

"This is basically what Christians have believed for thousands of years will happen in the last days, so I am not sharing anything new. But what is news is the fact that this is exactly what Harry suggested is now being planned and is about to be implemented by the elite. I believe we'll find more details on the flash drive."

"Any idea who the Messiah figure may be?" asked Marsha.

"I have a massive hunch when we see the information on the flash drive it will tell us who he is. Personally, I believe that man is the newly elected head of the European Union, Emmanuel Kohav."

At that moment Aaron's computer let out a beeping sound indicating it had finished decrypting the drive.

Chapter 17

Everyone rushed to Aaron's office to see what information was contained on the now decrypted flash drive.

They gathered around Aaron and gazed at the screen and gasped.

As he scrolled through the information, much of what Hal had been saying was confirmed.

Everyone was stunned into silence as images of Vatican officials, and Nazi leaders flashed across the screen.

Then images of Hitler himself with what appeared to be an alien being, gray in appearance with large black eyes, came into view.

So much was contained on the flash drive it took the better part of the day to wade through it all.

Fatima photographs never seen before showing the children kneeling in front of a floating globe of light drew gasps from the little group.

After several hours of viewing, their eyes became increasingly tired, and they were about to take a break when photographs of Emmanuel Kohav appeared.

These drew the sharpest intakes of breath as Kohav was pictured in a private audience with the newly elected Pope Julius and what appeared to be an alien.

What shocked everyone, even further was the fact that Pope Julius was kneeling in front of Kohav as the European President and the alien gray placed their hands upon the pontiff's head in an act of blessing.

They inspected the photograph for some minutes discussing what it could mean.

"To me the meaning is obvious," Hal said finally. "This confirms Kohav is the seed of Satan: the coming Antichrist. I believe this photograph is showing us very clearly Kohav and this demonic creature posing as an alien gray are commissioning Julius as the prophesied False Prophet of the book of Revelation. Why else would the Pope of Rome kneel before a politician and a creature like this gray? It just doesn't happen. This is an incredible photograph. No wonder they wanted Harry Langston dead."

"What is the document attached to the photograph, Aaron?"

Aaron opened the file while Tracey translated it from the French.

"The chosen seed and the lead alien brother

greeting and blessing Pope Julius in anticipation of the arrival of the divine spirit and its union with humankind due to be celebrated on April 30 at 8 p.m. at the CERN facility Geneva."

"That is it," Hal shouted. "Look at the date: three months time. I believe we have been given the very date when and where I believe the spirit from the bottomless pit of Revelation eleven will be released to enter Emmanuel Kohav making him the Antichrist of the last days.

"That vile creature you see there is a fallen angel, and it is him or his master who will enter Kohav and control the planet."

Marsha looked puzzled. "What bottomless pit are you talking about, Hal?"

"Excuse me, Marsha," he smiled. "In the book of Revelation, chapter eleven it mentions a being from a place called the bottomless pit being released on the earth. From then on throughout the book of Revelation, the person people regard as the Antichrist is called the beast from the bottomless pit.

"Now I am beginning to see what CERN is all about. We know they have been talking about opening different dimensions in the search for the so-called God particle: the source of the big bang that they believe created the known Universe. I suspect the spirit that will come from the bottomless pit will be the star turn at the up-coming CERN event with Kohav. Entering our world from another dimension, it will enter and control Emmanuel Kohav."

Jack pointed his finger in the air. "I am convinced, Hal but I am interested to learn if there is any other Biblical evidence Kohav is their golden boy?"

Aaron said, "I think this may help convince the doubters, Hal."

A graphic of Jerusalem was on the screen. Aaron pressed the play button, and the Temple Mount came into view as the graphic settled above the Muslim Dome of the Rock. In the empty area to the north of the Dome, building blocks appeared gradually forming the Jewish Temple.

"The Temple right beside the Dome of the Rock? Is that even possible?" Dinah asked.

Hal said, "Talks have been going on for the last few years between Muslims and the Jewish Sanhedrin regarding the original site of Solomon's Temple. This Temple you see here is the very Temple Antichrist will enter and desecrate according to two Thessalonians chapter two.

"I was amazed to watch a TV program a few weeks ago where they agreed that in the pursuit of peace the Temple beside the Dome of the Rock would be highly significant.

"The days ahead will bring a Middle East peace between Israel and the Palestinians, allowing them to build the Temple. Here is the very plan for such a Temple."

"This gets bigger by the moment," Aaron sighed. "How do we, this little group, combat something like this: Kohav and this creature from the pit; the entire Roman Catholic Church and very probably the whole ecumenical movement seeking a global spiritual brotherhood and a Temple in Jerusalem for the Antichrist to desecrate?"

"We can only do what God directs us to do. We certainly have a responsibility to inform as many who will listen." Hal sighed.

"I think we should settle down in the lounge and hear what else Hal has to say." Dinah waved her arm toward the door. "We have been here for the last few hours poring over this information, and I think we have a lot to talk about."

It was agreed, and Aaron went into the kitchen to make coffee while Dinah joined him and made a few sandwiches.

Once everyone was settled, Hal moved further into his subject. "Okay, let's look at Emmanuel Kohav. It's clear, from what we have been looking at he is the best candidate for the role of Antichrist. In fact, I think we should by now be convinced he will become the Antichrist.
Here are some more reasons for believing he is the man. Bible scholars for centuries have studied the scriptures regarding the Antichrist.

"One point that is often overlooked by modern teachers, but was preached by the early church is that the Antichrist is also known as the Assyrian. There is a prediction in the book of Micah that says Messiah will bring peace when the Assyrian treads down the land.

"Now verse two is a prediction about Messiah being born in Bethlehem. But verse five says he will be our peace when the Assyrian treads down our palaces.

"But, no Assyrian ruled Israel after the Messiah, Yeshua was born. So it has to be speaking of a later time, and many church fathers looked on this as a prediction of Messiah's rule after conquering the invading Assyrian. For this reason, they said Antichrist must also be the Assyrian mentioned in verse five. Also, it is clear from scripture Antichrist must be Jewish."

Marsha said, "Hal, you said Emmanuel Kohav will be the Antichrist. And you give us some interesting reasons to believe that. I was wondering, isn't he supposed to build the Temple or something? I remember hearing this on some TV show ages ago and thought it was interesting."

Hal nodded. "Yes, there is a belief the Antichrist will build the Temple and that adds more reasons for Kohav being the best choice at the moment. Certainly, as I said a moment ago, Antichrist is supposed to desecrate the Temple according to two Thessalonians chapter two verse four. Here," he opened his Bible and read. *Who opposeth and exalteth himself above all that is called God, or that is worshipped; so that he as God sitteth in the temple of God, shewing himself that he is God.*

"So it would seem he will oversee the building of a Jewish Temple in Jerusalem. Also, according to the scriptures in Daniel chapter nine, he will begin by allowing the ancient sacrificial system to begin, but after three and a half Biblical years he puts a stop to the sacrifices. Why he does that is debatable, but some conjecture this is the point he demands the people worship him instead of what the world by then will consider an outmoded form of worship to the God of the Bible."

"But why exactly would he do that?" asked Dinah as she joined in.

"Interesting question, Dinah," Hal replied.

"This is only my idea, but you will notice in Daniel eleven verse thirty-seven it says this," He flipped the pages of his Bible. *"Neither shall he regard the God of his fathers, nor the desire of women, nor regard any god: for he shall magnify himself above all."* He continued. "The term *God of his fathers* can be found throughout the Old Testament. It is distinctly Jewish which points to the Antichrist being Jewish. It then says in the next verse that he will honor the god of forces. The Hebrew word translated "forces" is "Mauzzim." Some commentators suggest this is related to a god of military might. But I was stunned when I did a study on this Hebrew word because as I did, I discovered the Turkish word for the one who calls people to pray to Allah is called a Muezzin."

"Do you see how close to the Hebrew word "Mauzzim," translated by many to mean "forces," is to the Turkish "Muezzin" the one who calls people to pray to Allah? The first word Mauzim is plural in Hebrew and the second is singular. Could it be the Jewish Antichrist will be an Assyrian Jew who will "not regard the God of his (Jewish) fathers" but instead "honor the god of (the) Muezzim" the ones who call people to pray to Allah, the god of Islam? I am no language expert, and this could easily be a fantastic coincidence. Time, again, will tell.

"But one other thing we know for sure: Kohav was born in Turkey. Turkey is part of the old Assyrian empire. He is an Assyrian Jew who now has very close contacts with Israel and Palestine through his friendship with the Israeli and Palestinian leadership. As a leading political figure in France for years, he has been trying to forge a peace deal between Israel and the Palestinians.

"Of course, being born in Turkey, he is also in close association with the Turkish leadership and has an affinity with Islam. What that bodes for the future cannot be good."

Jack scratched his head. "So does the European Union come into this mix or not?"

"Yes, it certainly does," Hal replied. "Daniel chapter two predicted the rise and fall of different empires before the Messiah returns and sets up his kingdom. What is absolutely fascinating is the fact this was written when

Babylon was the ruling world empire. Yet Daniel correctly predicted the empires that would follow Babylon's destruction down to the final one: a revived Roman Empire. That, I believe, is what we see today in the European Union. Somehow, in the near future, it will be the main player in the days running up to the return of Yeshua. And as we know Kohav is the head of the European Union."

"Okay, going back to the Temple, when will the Temple be built?" Jack asked as they dug into the sandwiches Dinah had just placed on the coffee table.

"We cannot be sure. However, the obvious place is the Temple Mount in Jerusalem. There have been ongoing arguments over the original location. But most Israeli archaeologists believe it was north of the Dome of the Rock in a large empty area on the Temple Mount, as we have just seen in the graphic. So it's obvious from what we have just watched, that is where the elite want it built for the Antichrist. Somehow they will fool the Israelis and the Muslims into going along with the plan.

"A while ago Rabbis decided if the Temple is to be erected it should be on this northern area alongside the Dome. At the moment it is all in the air with arguments from both sides, but it looks like it is very much on the cards of the secret rulers.

"Summing up: Emmanuel Kohav is Jewish, of Assyrian descent, but works hand in hand with the Vatican. He is the leader of the EU: the revived Roman Empire of Daniel's prophecy and has immense influence within the UN due to his Middle Eastern contacts as well as the Turkish and worldwide Islamic community, and his friends in the global elite who are working feverishly toward a global government. Also, we now know he is due to attend a ceremony at CERN headquarters. And what seals it has to be the photograph we have just seen with him and that abominable creature blessing the pope in anticipation of the CERN event. Also remember the pope is the first Jewish pope in two thousand years, if you believe Peter was the first pope, which I do not. They are working this together. How can any of us have any doubts Emmanuel Kohav is, or will very soon become the Antichrist?"

"When one researches Kohav's birth as I have done, it is shrouded in mystery. The father is unknown. There is a rumor Kohav's mother belonged to a very influential group of occultists gathered from the world of politics, religion, science and so on.

"There is an apparently unconfirmed story that she was impregnated by Satan himself during a high occult celebration known as the Feast of the Beast. Two people died around the time of the feast, which coincidentally was nine months before Kohav was born. One of them was the chauffeur and personal assistant to Kohav's mother.

"My contacts did some poking around and discovered Kohav's mother and this assistant stayed at a Hotel in the South of France around the time she would have become pregnant. The assistant was seen with a young woman who, I am given to understand, left the building with him in a hurry. The bar steward, who is now retired, told my agent, he believed he heard the assistant coaxing the young lady to follow his boss, the future mummy Kohav."

"Did this guy tell the authorities what he knew when these two people turned up dead?"

"The mother was, and still is, the Countess de Mourney. She owned the Hotel; still does, I believe. It was put to the bar steward in unambiguous language; *you want to keep your job, pour drinks or else another tragic accident can be arranged, so shut your mouth*, and he did just that. Now he's old, dying of cancer wants to make his peace with God and doesn't care."

Jack spoke. "So you believe the Countess became pregnant with Kohav as a direct result of a sexual encounter with the Devil during the Feast of the Beast? What a foul detestable thing to do."

"Sounds crazy, but yes, I do believe it, without a doubt," replied Hal gravely. "If fallen angels impregnated women back in Genesis, why couldn't Satan himself father the ultimate rebel? And now it is clear the Vatican, the global elite and these fallen entities from beyond are working hand in hand to bring things to a head in the near future at CERN."

Jack closed his eyes. He asked "Could you expand on something else for us unenlightened ones, please? How deep is the link between the Vatican and these creatures? I am having a real problem processing all this information."

"Certainly," Hal gave a deep sigh. "The Catholic Church has been watching UFOs for a little over three hundred years. They have their own observatory beside the pope's summer residence in Castle Gandolfo in Italy. They also have an observatory on Mount Graham in Arizona, where they not only observe the heavens but UFO activity as well. Believe it or not, Mount Graham is a traditional American Indian holy site. They believe a portal exists there to the world of the fallen angels. Though of course, they would never believe that is what these beings they contact really are."

Jack opened his mouth to speak, but Hal held his hand up and continued. "Back in two thousand and nine, Pope Benedict held a conference at the Vatican with more than thirty astronomers, physicists, biologists and other experts to discuss extraterrestrial life: aliens!

"In the year two thousand, Vatican theologian Monsignor Balducci was featured on Italian national television where he said alien contact was real and alien beings are his brothers.

"Over the years at various times, Vatican observers have paid visits to the CERN headquarters in Switzerland. I would guess they will not want to miss being present at the special ceremony that is coming up. From what we have just read what is due to take place there will be monumental."

Chapter 18

The next morning as they sat at breakfast, Lauren asked, "Hal, how will we know what goes on at the CERN ceremony in April?"

Hal smiled and winked. "Well, we know from the flash drive there will be a kind of demonic impartation involving Kohav and probably a fallen angel." He smiled. "But, my dear, thanks to Aaron's electronic bag of tricks, he now has two passes for us. They are not completely authorized passes, but they should get two of us into the ceremony."

"Passes?" Dinah asked. "When did you sneakily do that, Aaron?"

Her husband put his arm around her shoulders and squeezed. "Last night while you were asleep. Hal pulled me to one side as we came in here to pray and asked if it was possible. Of course, it's simplicity itself to create a card on my program if you know just what kind you are looking for and know what buttons to press." He chuckled. "So I waited until you were asleep, ran a few searches and found the passes needed for this meeting."

"*Us?*" Jack interrupted. "What do you mean by "*us*," Hal, and "*they are not completely authorized passes*?"

"Okay, they are fake, of course, created by Aaron but good enough to get through security. Who's game for this?"

Jack's hand shot into the air, "I'm in."

"A reporter to the last," Hal laughed out loud. "And I think the whizz kid, Aaron should be the number two in case of problems."

"Count me in." Smiled Aaron, while Dinah grimaced.

"I don't like this idea." She said.

"Me neither," Marsha joined in.

"It will be fine, darling. Just in and out. No problem." Aaron tried to reassure his wife.

Jack looked at Marsha, who avoided his smile. "Marsha, honey. Aaron's right. It will be an in and out job. We'll witness what goes on and skedaddle out and away."

"I know I can't stop you, but I can't hide my fears. This is very hazardous territory. It isn't just the human side. We know there is also an area we have never come across until these last few days."

"If you don't want me to go I'll let Hal go in my place."

"And regret not letting you do your job? No way. Just come back to me." She forced a smile and turned away. Even though it pained her, Marsha wouldn't stop him for the world from doing what he loved.

Hal nodded. "So that's settled, we can spend the next few weeks making plans for getting you into the CERN facility for the ceremony and hopefully plan a way of escape should everything suddenly go pear-shaped and you get yourselves into any problems."

"If everything hits the fan and we get caught there will be little we can do about it. It's a risk I am afraid we'll have to take." Jack said resignedly.

Hal nodded. "This is so important. The whole world is being played like a finely tuned violin. As I said yesterday, our leaders, or should I say the puppeteers behind the scenes, who want global governance, are not stupid, mindless morons. More chaos equals more fear, equals more control, equals less personal freedom, equals the coming of big brother and the Antichrist. Remember the saying ordo ab chao: order out of chaos or better still, create a problem to solve a problem."

Hal leaned forward and clasped his hands together as if in prayer.

"The very spirit of Antichrist, the beast from the bottomless pit will soon be released on the earth. Emmanuel Kohav will become the Antichrist, of that, we are as good as certain.

"Jack and Aaron will be there to bear witness to the diabolical event. I fully believe what takes place beneath CERN will provide us with the final piece of evidence we need.

"The beast from the bottomless pit will somehow interact with or enter Emmanuel Kohav, and he will become the Antichrist. You must be on your guard every second you are there. One error and they will see to it you never leave the place."

"So, what do we do in the meantime?" Asked Marsha, who didn't want to hear about the possible dangers her husband would soon be facing.

Hal stood up from the settee. "We must begin to plan for the days ahead. How we are to travel to Switzerland, where to stay and how to leave when we need to."

"Surely we don't all have to travel there, do we?" asked Aaron. "Only Jack and I need to go. Surely the rest of us should stay here where it's safe."

"I think it's better if we are not divided," Hal replied. "If something goes wrong and we are hundreds of miles apart, we could be sitting here while they research Jack and Aaron's movements and history. Before we knew it, they would be after us. At least if we are close and, God forbid, they don't make it back to us, we can move immediately. Where we are now is our best safe house, but once they track Aaron's file, they'd be on the doorstep."

"Can't we move to a safer place?" Asked Lauren.

"Where would you suggest, Lauren? Here we are out of the way and almost off the grid. But if the detain Aaron and conduct a thorough search into his history, they will know he and Dinah have this place, and they'd be here within hours while we wait for a signal from Aaron and Jack. But if we are in Geneva close by and they don't return we can move quickly to the airport and get away."

"I don't see the difference. We don't know how long the meeting will last do we, so how can we know when to expect a signal from Aaron to say all is okay?"

"We can be pretty certain if we don't hear anything by one to two in the morning we should move." Hal countered.

Dinah suddenly joined in. "I have no intention of letting Aaron go flying off into the wild blue yonder without me, I am going with him as far as possible, and I don't care what anyone else says."

"That goes for me too," chimed Marsha. "No

way is my husband going into danger without me being as close as possible."

Hal laughed, "Wow. That's settled then. We all go to Geneva together. Let's sit down and plan."

Chapter 19

Lord Haldane entered the chamber. Secreted beneath the streets of London, it was huge dank and dark. The few lights positioned around the cavernous walls shed eerie shadows across the floor. The chamber was already full with the other members of the committee who had taken their seats in ascending rows. He took his place at the head of the room facing the others as if he was a lecturer about to address his students.

"Fellow members of the Committee, I am aware most of you know of the recent events involving the copying onto a flash drive of the list of members, our conversations, plans for the coming world leader and most damning of all, the names of those who opposed us and have since been eliminated. A move I am afraid we may come to regret unless this little group of opposers, who hold this and other information, is dealt with and dealt with swiftly."

Sir Harold Gray spoke. "Haldane, the committee gave you full powers to deal with this problem. What went wrong? Why isn't it resolved?"

Haldane stammered."I...I am afraid those to

whom I entrusted the task failed miserably. First, the botched affair at the Abbey, then the failed apprehension of Jack Bridger in the center of London and following that, the being I summoned to prevent him escaping with the flash drive...all failed. Following that the attempt to kidnap Bridger's wife also met with unexpected results. We then planned to kill them by occult means again, as they drove through the countryside. As you are aware, several of us met in this very hall to call up the force that we believed would kill them. This was also met with spiritual defeat at the hands of their God."

"Five failed attempts. One could be looked upon as simple bad luck, but five is downright unforgivable incompetence."

Haldane clenched his jaws in anger "May I remind you, sir, to whom you are speaking?" His voice raised in a fury of self-defense.

"I know exactly who you are, sir. You are supposed to be the head of this section of the committee. But your reckless actions have opened us to complete exposure. You planned each of these failed attempts. Therefore, it is you who are responsible for their failure. The incompetents you chose for the tasks remain your responsibility. You are incapable of leading this section of the committee. You have placed us in the utmost danger of exposure on the eve of the event of the ages: something our forebears and we throughout the centuries have planned and worked for. Some gave their very lives to further the grand scheme: the emergence of the first emperor of the planet, empowered by our Lord Lucifer."

Haldane stepped forward to plead his case, but Grey held his hand aloft. "Enough of your failures and your puny excuses, Haldane. You are not fit to be a part of this illustrious group let alone lead it. We believed you would be able to carry out the desires of the committee. Unfortunately, we were wrong."

Haldane pleaded. "Sirs, I realize my errors in trusting the work to others less able to perform the tasks. The being that was summoned and the globe of death that was sent to finish them, though powerful, were both thwarted by the intervention of the God of the Christians. Surely..."

He was cut short as a man, who had been sitting quietly in the front of the assembly, rose to his feet. Haldane visibly shrunk back as the man stepped forward.

"President Kohav. Sir, I..."

"What, Lord Haldane? What were you about

to say?" Kohav purred softly. A sadistic smile crept across his lips.

"President Kohav I did not know you would be here."

"Really? Didn't you think I would wish to hear your excuses for your useless attempts to secure the flash drive? To myself and our gathered friends, you seem to have done all in your power to prevent my accession to the position that has been prepared for me since the Garden of Eden, rather than work to bring it to pass. Thanks be to Lucifer, although I am not in full possession of my soon to be inherited powers from my father, I do have some abilities."

"Sir, Mister President..."

"We have no need of failures, Haldane."

Kohav stepped forward and placed his hand on Haldane's chest. "No need whatsoever." His eyes grew dark and menacing.

The helpless and terrified Haldane tried to remove Kohav's hand, but it was like a solid rock, pressing into his chest. His face began to redden as his chest began to swell. Kohav slowly raised his hand away as if drawing Haldane toward him. The hapless Peer's eyes bulged, and he gasped for breath, then screamed as his shirt ripped open revealing his naked chest. His skin swelled and suddenly burst, releasing a torrent of blood as his heart was torn from his body. He fell lifeless to the floor.

"Remove him," Kohav ordered. "Now, Gentlemen, to business. Who shall we elect as the new head of this section of the committee? Any volunteers?" He smiled as he wiped the blood from his hands.

Chapter 20

Emmanuel Kohav paced the floor of his private office in the European Union Parliament building in Brussels. Since his election as EU president two months earlier, the former president of France had seized the reins of his new position with vigor. His mother, the Assyrian Jewess, Countess de Mourney had used her immense influence over former lovers and associates, to ensure her son won the election by stealth, lies, and threats. She was also the driving force behind his vigorous campaign schedule that won the hearts and minds of the electorate.

He had taken the name Kohav out of respect for his Assyrian Jewish ancestry, but also to distance himself from his mother's questionable past while seeing to it she orchestrated his election campaign from the shadows. The results had been stupendous. A landslide victory against all the opposition had given Kohav a sixty percent lead over his nearest rival for the top post.

Emmanuel Kohav was indeed the man of the hour.

After appearing to be a rising star in French politics and winning the French presidency, he had suffered a humiliating defeat in the vote for a second term. As a result, he faded from public view for three years. But he and his small team had not been idle. While continuing to work discreetly within European politics, he had gradually gained notable popularity. With the help of his mother's contacts, they had launched a comeback fight that had now catapulted Kohav into the position of the head of the EU.

The European Union, the joining together of the nations of the former Roman Empire, had been the dream of politicians, popes, kings, emperors, and dictators for centuries. From the crowning of Charlemagne by Pope Leo III on Christmas day in the year 800 with the accompanying proclamation making him emperor of the Holy Roman Empire, through to Napoleon and finally Adolph Hitler and his Third Reich or Third Empire: Rome being the first and the Holy Roman Empire, the second.

Although the world knew this marriage of nations as the European Union, behind closed doors, it was also known as the Revived Roman Empire or Project Babylon.

But what so many also failed to see behind the elite's game of smoke and mirrors was the fact that the Vatican and its Roman Catholic servants had been pulling the strings from the decline of the Roman empire to the present day. They even went so far as to help Nazi war criminals escape to South America with new identities, in readiness to return to power and fight the Communists should Russia take over the whole of Europe after the war. It would appear Rome would rather do all in her power to establish a European Socialist empire than a Communist one.

After the war, moves were made, principally by Catholic politicians, to bring about a brotherhood of Europe by creating a Superstate with its own Parliament, monetary system, anthem, Court of Justice and even its own army, though it was never sold to the public as such.

Those who were politically awake saw immediately what was being planned. Those who were spiritually aware knew the rabbit hole went much deeper than simple politics and the desire to unite age-old enemies in peaceful co-existence.

What was being laid was the foundation for the eventual fulfillment of ancient Hebrew prophecies from the Bible. Soon the world would witness the rise of the Antichrist and his political empire and the appearance of the one who would spiritually deceive the masses: the False Prophet of the book of Revelation.

This deceiver would lead the false religious system of the last days called the Whore of Babylon and Babylon the Great. This diabolical duo would take the world into the period known as the Great Tribulation.

Incredibly, the EU Parliament building was modeled on a painting of the Tower of Babel (Babylon) by Dutch artist Pieter Bruegel. Just as God was said to have destroyed the Tower of Babel in Genesis chapter eleven, the Parliament building gave the false impression of being partly completed.

In the front of the building stood the statue of the goddess Europa of Greek mythology, sitting upon the back of the god Saturn or Zeus after he disguised himself as a bull and carried her away to be raped.

Many Christian students of Bible prophecy viewed the EU, the building and the statue as prophetic signs of the last days of world history, due to take shape before the rise of the Antichrist's empire: the final empire before the physical return to earth of Jesus Christ.

The Revived Roman Empire, Babylon and the Woman riding the Beast (the Whore of Babylon) were predicted in the Old Testament book of Daniel and later in chapters seventeen and eighteen of the New Testament book of Revelation. And here they stood in plain sight for the world to see: a divine warning of what was to come. But so few realized the embryo of fulfilled Bible prophecy was staring them in the face.

Now it was time for Emmanuel Kohav to begin the next phase of his rise to power within this Revived Roman Empire of the last days: the uniting of Palestinians and Israelis.

He went to his desk and pressed the intercom. His secretary answered immediately. "Yes, sir?"

"Michelle, update me, please, on the Israeli President's progress?"

"His plane landed just five minutes ago, sir, he should be here in about thirty-five minutes. As soon as his security lets me know they are ten minutes away I shall call you. The press is simply everywhere, and our welcome delegation is already moving into position awaiting your presence."

"Very well. Thank you."

He went to the restroom, combed his thick black hair, straightened his tie and looked at himself in the mirror. "Emmanuel, this is it. The time has come."

Fifteen minutes later, amid a flurry of

paparazzi, flashing cameras, microphones being thrust in his face and cries of "Over here, Mister President," reporters vied with each other to be the first to get a comment from President Kohav as the Israeli president arrived. His black, bullet-proof limo pulled up directly in front of Emmanuel Kohav and the leaders of the EU member states awaiting his arrival. Several accompanying limousines drew up behind that of the president, the entire motorcade coming to a halt at the same time.

Several Israeli security men jumped from the second limo and surrounded the one carrying President Shlomo Goren. One security team had arrived a day earlier and were stationed almost invisibly at various vantage points in and around the Parliament buildings.

After looking carefully around and getting the okay in their earpieces, the president's bodyguards opened the back doors of the limo, and President Goren and his wife Eva stepped out into the late summer sunshine. Both in their late fifties, but looking slim and healthy, the president and his wife were warmly greeted by Kohav and his entourage.

The cameras snapped, and the reporters yelled for a few words as Kohav, the Israeli Head Of State and his wife stood for a few moments.

"President Kohav, will you be discussing the present situation in the Middle East?"

"President Goren and I will be covering a number of topics over the next couple of days during the president and Misses Oren's brief visit. We hope to make a joint statement then."

Kohav guided his guests into the Parliament building where they were greeted by the rousing cheers of the delegates gathered in the main assembly hall.

A female assistant directed the Israeli president's wife to her seat while her husband, accompanied by Emmanuel Kohav, stepped to the front of the Assembly Hall and took their seats beside the Assembly Chairman, facing the applause of the delegates.

The chairman raised his hands for quiet as Emmanuel Kohav stepped to the dais and stood ready to address the gathered throng.

"Fellow Europeans, since the close of the Second World War the world has witnessed many changes, many tragedies and many joys intertwined through the years. The dream of world peace has sometimes seemed as elusive as a vapor: something impossible to grasp as a reality. Even today we are witnesses to many tensions in various quarters of the planet.

"At present, there has been no worse tragedy,

no problem of our modern era that has so plagued the minds of men longer than the division of brothers in the Middle East. The Israeli and Palestinian quest for a peaceful solution to their decades-old search for justice, peace and security for both sides has been splattered with the blood of the guilty and the innocent, and there seems to be no end in sight to the problems they face as they search for a lasting settlement to their differences.

"In the past, many have attempted to help create what at the time turned out to be impossible: peace in the Middle East. Today we continue, steadfastly working to build bridges of peace between these two ancient peoples from whose lands the world's two largest religions have sprung. I speak, of course, of Islam and Christianity.

"Many of you gathered here today are devoted members of the Roman Catholic Church. It must be remembered the faith you follow had its genesis in the Middle East. So what better place on earth should there be to find peace? But instead, we discover violence, hatred, and mistrust. This has to end and end now.

"We intend over the coming months and years to do our utmost to bring together in peace and security once and for all time, these two brothers who have been separated for far too long. We are at this moment formulating a peace covenant between the two parties that will initially run for several years until renewed.

"Like the prodigal son, Israel has come home but has found no peace with his brother and the brother has found no peace with the prodigal son. Both want the land, the inheritance of the father. With the aid of the Divine eternal spirit, we intend to encourage them and help them with every resource at our disposal, to share the land, the inheritance together in peace and security.

"Therefore, as a foretaste of our desire to help bring peace to this troubled region, it is my esteemed privilege and honor at this time, to welcome to the European Union and this podium, his Excellency Shlomo Goren, President of the State of Israel.

Goren stepped toward the dais and shook Kohav's hand, and the two hugged one another. Kohav gestured for Oren to speak and took his seat.

The welcoming applause died, and Oren cleared his throat.

"President Kohav, your excellencies, presidents, prime ministers and honored officials of the European Union. On behalf of the Jewish people and the nation of Israel, I thank you for your generous welcome offered to myself and my wife. I bid you Shalom from Israel and her eternal capital city of Jerusalem.

"Words cannot express the thankfulness I hold in my heart toward you all at this time. As no doubt you are all aware of the ongoing problems raging to our north in Syria and the continued threats we receive from Lebanon from parties such as Hezbollah, Islamic Jihad and of course, Iran, which not only issues threats to annihilate Israel but has now also moved its elite forces into areas no more than thirty kilometres from Israel's northern border.

"In our south, we have continued threats and even missiles entering Israel from Gaza which is the stronghold of Hamas. I am sure many of you know the very name Hamas means violence in Hebrew. It is from this name many Israelis take comfort from our prophet Yeshayahu or as you know him, Isaiah. In chapter sixty verse eighteen the Lord promised Israel a coming day when violence will no longer be heard in the land. The prophet uses the very same word in Hebrew for violence: Hamas.

"The Lord says there will be a day when

Hamas is no longer heard in the land of Israel. We long for that day. A day when no violence of any kind will be heard from the south, east or north of Israel. A day when we can indeed live in peace with our neighbors. So, I am profoundly grateful to all gathered here, but especially to President Kohav and his excellent team, all of you who have extended such a warm invitation and welcome to visit the center of the European Union at what we pray will be a pivotal time in the history of the Middle East.

"We are greatly encouraged in recent days, by the new leadership in Saudi Arabia and the friendly overtures for co-operation we have received from them. Also, our common ground regarding the war in Syria and concern over Russia's growing role in Middle Eastern affairs.

"We also find mutual concern regarding the growing threats from Russia's ally, Iran against both Israel and the EU. These are early days, but our hope is that perhaps, a united front against Iran's belligerence will pour water on what could be the fuse that would ignite the region into a major conflict. That is something, of course, no one wants to see. Especially as we are doing all in our power to form a dialogue for a Two-State solution with Jerusalem as the capital not of Israel alone but of both Israel and Palestine.

"Israel does not, of course, forget or exclude, in any way, our dear ally the United States in all these negotiations and President Charles Martin whose tireless efforts for peace we honor. But we live in hope and pray for peace.

"My wife and I look forward to many years of profitable and fruitful cooperation between the European Union and the State of Israel.

"Once again, I thank you for your kind welcome and support in our mutual search for a peaceful and lasting solution to the differences we encounter with our Arab and Palestinian neighbors. Thank you so much."

The gathered heads of state stood to their feet and applauded in appreciation of the Israeli President's articulate presentation on behalf of his nation.

The two leaders again shook hands and stepped toward the hallway leading to Kohav's office and stateroom where they were to be interviewed and photographed by the world press.

Seated in the stateroom Kohav and Oren shook hands for the press photo opportunity.

Questions came bullet-like, thick and fast.

"How do you see the future of Israeli relations with the European Union?"

"Does Israel hope to increase any business expansion within the EU? Oren replied, to laughter "I am a Jewish businessman, what kind of an answer do you expect? Yes, we hope many technological enterprises created in Israel will find further ground for development within the European Union as they have done in the USA, Canada and elsewhere. I believe there are great opportunities for trade in both directions: to Israel and from Israel. This is something we hope to discuss in the coming days. "

"You mentioned the war in Syria and alluded to Russia's role in Middle Eastern affairs. Could you expand on that for us? Do you anticipate Russian interference either politically or militarily?"

"Russia is doing both already. They support the present regime in Syria, which is anti-Israel. The Russian government is also bonding with Turkey, which is likewise pro-Palestinian and anti-Israel.

"The Russian's are solid supporters of Iran, also would like nothing better than to see a mushroom cloud over Tel Aviv. So, even though Israel is on friendly terms with Russia at present, the situation could change in a moment if we do not take extreme care. As I am sure, you all know, in recent hours Russian, Iranian and Turkish forces have gathered on the border of northern Syria. We have had no communications with the Russians and their allies for the last twenty-four hours.

"The IDF is continually monitoring the situation, but I have to tell you it doesn't look very hopeful. I was pressed to cancel my visit here today, but to my mind, that doesn't help or hinder the situation. Prime Minister Ben-Asher has my complete trust, and I know he will do whatever becomes necessary to protect the State of Israel should it come to that. We hope beyond hope that this is merely sabre-rattling on behalf of Israel's enemies.

"We do live in perilous times as I believe your New Testament warns regarding the last days. Many of our respected Rabbis believe we are in those days too. But they expect the Messiah to come for the first time and deliver us from such a catastrophic scenario as a full-blown Middle East war. Christians are expecting a Messiah who will come a second time. When he does arrive we will have to ask "is this your first or second visit to Israel, sir?" There was polite, laughter in response to Goren's joke.

"Do you believe in the Messiah, sir?"

Goren looked down for a moment, "Young lady, I have lived almost too long. I have seen loved ones killed on the streets of Jerusalem. My grandparents were in Dachau and died there during the Holocaust. My mother was there also and lost her faith in a Jewish Messiah coming to rescue her after watching her mother die of typhus and her father starve to death. She arrived in Israel or Palestine as it was then, as a survivor, weak and barely able to walk. She met my father who was a Sabra, a homegrown Jew born in the land.

"As I grew up, hearing her tell of life in the camps, I inherited her lack of faith. But when I met President Kohav, and witnessed his hard work and deep, sincere desire to see peace between Israel and Palestine, even before he became president of the EU, hope sprang again, and right now," he paused. "I am beginning to wonder, if Messiah really is, at last, on his way, or," he looked inquiringly into Emmanuel Kohav's eyes. "If he is not here already."

Suddenly, without warning, alarms were sounding off all over the building. A security man ran toward Kohav and Goren accompanied by Kohav's secret service men and the Israeli security team. They virtually scooped Goran and Kohav off their chairs and rushed them along with the president's wife, down the hallway to an elevator and then down several stories beneath ground level.

"What on earth is happening?" Goren gasped. The Israeli team leader spoke in Hebrew. "Sir, we have reports of missiles preparing to be launched from silos in Russia. We cannot ascertain if this is a drill or where they are being directed. We must make you secure."

Chapter 21

"Jack, Jack," the voice was urgent, and the knocking on the bedroom door was insistent.

Jack rolled out of bed and opened the door.

Hal burst in. "Jack, you'd better come downstairs. Grab Marsha too. While we've been fighting and running from the Devil, it looks like World War Three is about to break out."

Jack threw on a loose top and still bare-footed and in his shorts, he followed Hal down to the lounge. Marsha dressed and followed a minute or two later.

Everyone else was already sitting watching the huge TV screen in Aaron's and Dinah's lounge.

"What's happened?" Jack asked.

"Seems the war in Syria has spilled over into Israel. The problem is Russia. The Russians have mobilized their forces and Iran and Turkey have joined them."

"And their purpose at present is what?" Marsha asked.

"From what the reports are saying, Russia has accused Israel and Saudi Arabia of ganging up on Syria and Lebanon and the terrorist groups there. Iran already has troops in Syria. They have been itching to get at Israel for years and so has Turkey.

"Now Israel and Saudi Arabia have normalized relations, Iran and Russia are probably eyeing Middle Eastern oil fields as well as the massive gas and oil deposits Israel has discovered. They are using the fact that Israel retaliated by sending their army into southern Lebanon to clear out the factions that have been firing rockets into northern Israel.

"Russia has been warning Israel not to invade Lebanon, and now they have done, the Russians and Iranians have their reason for attacking Israel.

"Turkey has seen this as an opportunity to show solidarity with Russia and Iran and has joined forces with them, hoping to move into Israel and Saudi and pick up the spoils of war."

"What about the States? America has always promised to stand by Israel."

"Yes. Especially since President Trump sided with Israel calling Jerusalem their capital city and moved the American embassy from Tel Aviv to Jerusalem. President Martin has warned the Russians not to cross the red line."

"What red line?" asked Dinah, who had quickly dressed in her jogger bottoms and a loose top.

"The red line in this case," said Hal "is the Golan Heights, Israel's northern buffer zone. If the Russians or her allies step on the Golan, all bets are off. Let's get online and see what news is coming from the States.

Dinah turned on the live news from America. "This is KWM News Service with John Cremo reporting." Cremo sat behind the news desk looking worried. "Good morning. This is John Cremo reporting live from Washington. The escalating situation in Syria and Israel has just taken an even more ominous turn.

"News coming out of Jerusalem's national security and military centers have reported Russian, Turkish and Iranian troop movements in southern Lebanon, crossing toward the Golan Heights. We also have reports that in a recent telephone conversation with Russian President Kuznetsov. President Martin was told by the Russian premier not to interfere in the current situation. A source not wishing to be identified stated that in the middle of the exchange the Russian premier warned the American president in chilling terms never heard in recent history that American troops would meet their maker if they set an aggressive foot in Syria or Lebanon.

"At the same time, we have reports coming in

starting that Turkish, Iranian and Russian ships are now in the Mediterranean heading directly for Israel.

"From the White House, President Martin and his National Security team, as well as top military advisors, have been in conference. The DEFCON level has been set to DEFCON 3 which means the situation is serious enough for the Air Force if needed to be fully mobilized in just fifteen minutes."

Cremo held his hand to his earpiece as new information came in. "We take you directly to the White House, where President Martin is about to address the nation."

For a moment the screen went black then President Charles Martin appeared looking tired and drawn.

"My fellow Americans. I am speaking to you directly from the Situation Room beneath the White House. I want you to listen to me very carefully indeed. And make sure your loved ones and neighbors are aware of what I am about to say.

"Today I have warned Russian president Kuznetsov of the grave consequences he and his military advisors are embarking upon as they lead what has been a shock military mobilization and a reckless confederation of nations against our ally the State and the people of Israel. I have warned and pleaded with the Russian leadership to act with caution in this very delicate and potentially dangerous situation, but as many of you are by now aware I have received nothing but threats in return.

"In my most recent conversation with President Kuznetsov just five minutes ago I attempted to be conciliatory and sought, with the help of my national security advisors, to heal any rifts between our countries and see if we can call a halt to the Russian, Iranian and Turkish advance and set up an emergency international peace conference. As Russia is the leader of this confederation, I hoped against hope that he and his allies, with whom I have also been in contact, would listen to reason. I have to tell you, they have replied with threats to attack the USA if we take one step toward defending Israel.

"You know I campaigned in the presidential elections to protect you and our allies from all aggressors, including Iran and the growing threat from the Russian Federation as it made expansive moves into the Middle East.

"Even as far back as the year two thousand, we knew Russia was building permanent sea and military bases in Syria.

"From the moment of my election to this high office, I, as your president, promised once again, to protect you, and we as an administration and nation promised to protect and defend our allies around the world, including Israel, should the day dawn when they called upon us to come to their aid. That day has arrived as a double-edged sword hanging over our heads.

"To protect Israel means we shall be at war with Russia and those who band together and run to join this anti-Israel anti-American confederation now forming before our eyes. If we do not defend Israel at this time, I am reliably informed it is very likely the invading forces will also head for, and take over, the oil fields of the whole Middle East. Saudi Arabia, alone, has almost one-fifth of the world's proven oil reserves and ranks as the largest producer and exporter of oil in the world. The United States imports around sixty percent of our oil needs. Much of this comes from Canada. But a vast amount is imported from the Middle East. Were the Russians and Iranians and their allies to take over the Middle Eastern oil fields it would reduce many Western nations, if not all, to serfdom under the Russian bear and its partners in crime.

"Our own oil supplies alone would never sustain our present way of life. We would very soon be on our way to becoming a Third World nation dependent upon the kindness of Russia and her allies to supply the oil we need to continue to live up to the standard we enjoy at this present time.

"If we do defend Israel in this, her hour of need, and the unthinkable happens, and we lose the war, we could find ourselves in the same position or with God's help we could be the victors in the battle for what we believe to be a right and just cause.

"Therefore, I am telling you now, my dear friends and fellow Americans, we shall defend ourselves and Israel from these aggressors, come what may. They are on the move, and as you know from their history and rhetoric, they will not stop until the entire region is under their dominion and the Jewish people are dead or exiled from their homeland. We cannot, I cannot, allow this to happen and I fully intend to fulfill my promise to them and you.

"We pray with all our hearts such a nightmarish scenario will be avoided and common sense will prevail. But if not, let it be known we will enter any such confrontation as a last resort, but with determination to see it through to victory for the right.

"May God bless you, may God bless Israel, and may God bless the United States of America."

The screen reverted to the studio where Anchorman John Cremo was hurriedly skipping through his notes.

"We take you now to our reporter Brian Hadley in Jerusalem. Brian, what can you tell us about the current mood of the Israelis and their leadership?"

Brian Hadley appeared standing on the Mount of Olives with the Temple Mount in the background. "John, the situation here is extremely tense, as you may expect. The general population has been told to head for the shelters the moment they hear the warning sirens. Also, over the last few days the military has been mobilized and on full alert.

"Reservists have been called up, and all leave has been canceled.

"The last we heard, large units of ground forces, that means armed Israeli ground units as well as tanks and anti-aircraft and anti-missile units, have been heading toward the north of the country. The Air Force is patrolling the skies more than normal of course and operation Iron Dome; the Israeli anti- missile detection unit has been fully operational in case of any incoming projectiles.

"Since then, that was yesterday; there has been a total news blackout. I would assume intelligence sources connected to the USA and our allies would be receiving more up to date information."

"Has there been any sign of panic among Israelis at all?"

"Lots of panic buying of supplies like water and tinned food. Most of the food stores have virtually empty shelves right now. Even the Hotel myself and the team are staying in has reduced the daily food output. Whereas there used to be huge buffet breakfasts and evening meals these have been drastically reduced to conserve stores for guests.

"We have all been taken through drills and shown where the bomb-proof shelters are beneath our Hotel and nearby buildings should we be taken by surprise while outside. Apart from that, no actual panic by the Israelis.

"Last evening I went to the Western Wall, also known as the Wailing Wall, beside the Temple Mount. I was very moved indeed by the sight of literally thousands of Israelis, men, women, and children crammed into the plaza right up to the wall itself, praying for peace. Many

Rabbis calling for God to send the Messiah to deliver them. As I said, it was a very tense and moving experience. Most of these people have nowhere to go. This is their home. They have roots here and no family outside Israel.

"One elderly Rabbi told me with tears in his eyes, only God himself can save Israel. He said this is the Gog and Magog war predicted in the Biblical book of Ezekiel and as far as he is concerned, God will rescue them but at a cost to so many on both sides.

"The entire coalition now forming consists of Russia, which the Ezekiel chapter thirty-eight prophecy calls Gog and Magog, Turkey, which equates on ancient maps of the Middle East as Meshech, Tubal, Gomer, and the House of Togarmah. Persia, which, of course, is modern-day Iran and some would say Hezbollah. Ethiopia, in the prophecy, is modern day Sudan and Somalia, and finally Libya.

"Interestingly, most of the "Free Syrian Army" is composed of Libyans." Many are convinced what we are witnessing is for sure the beginning of the Gog, Magog war.

"Also, as I was speaking today to..." his voice trailed off as in the background, sirens began to wail out a warning of incoming missiles.

"We have sirens going off all over the city, and

we have been told to get down in the shelters, John. This is Brian Hadley, from Jerusalem." The screen went black.

"Thanks, Brian, stay safe." Cremo sat stunned for a few moments as he gathered himself together. His voice shook.

"Ladies and Gentlemen that was our reporter Brian Hadley live from Jerusalem, where it would appear an air attack on Israel of some description is underway at this moment. Please stay tuned as we will keep you updated as soon as any further news comes in."

He held his hand again to his earpiece.

"As you may already be aware, it seems we also have multiple alarms going off across the USA as I speak. If you are anywhere near a shelter, we advise you to get there right away. This is not a drill. I repeat this is not a drill. Get to a place of safety immediate...". The lights dimmed, then went bright again and the studio shook violently knocking lights and cameras to the floor. The force of the shock wave threw Cremo forward, and he cracked his head on the desk and fell unconscious. The studio lights flickered and went out completely. In the darkness, someone screamed, and the screen changed to white static.

Chapter 22

Israeli Prime Minister Yitzhak Ben-Asher turned to one of his aides. "Get the American President on the line. We need to get an immediate update on American troop movements to counter the Russian advance."

"I am sorry, sir," the aide's voice quavered.

"There is absolutely no signal from the USA."

The Israeli Situation Room buried twenty stories deep beneath the city of Tel Aviv, fell deathly still.

"What do you mean no signal from the USA?"

"Sir, there are absolutely no signals whatsoever emanating from within the borders of the United States."

"None...none at all?" Ben-Asher tilted his head to one side as he looked with disbelief at his assistant.

He had been Israel's most popular Prime Minister for the last four years, but this was the greatest test of his entire life, and it showed in the gray face and the deep worry lines that seemed to have appeared almost overnight.

The aide shook his head. "None at all, sir."

General David Arens said, "Sir, I am receiving reports of multiple missiles bursting over the U.S. mainland."

"Nuclear?"

"Sir, they seem to be nuclear, landing in major cities as well as EMPs detonating above strategic areas. The missiles were launched from Russia but also from previously undetected Russian subs off the East and West coasts of the USA. Somehow they managed to cloak the submarines from any radar detection. "What are you telling us, General?"

Arens took a sharp intake of breath.

"To put it bluntly, sir, the entire American nation has effectively just been castrated.

"The Nuclear explosions and the electromagnetic pulse missiles detonating above the USA appear to have sent the United States of America back to the early 1800's: practically no electricity of any kind, whatsoever. It's as if they have suddenly reverted to the days of the Wild West.

"There were some successes we understand. Part of the National Grid was protected from the EMPs but then crashed. Virtually, their entire communication system will have been fried. Their computers, phones, landlines, and cell phones, cars, planes and so on, as well as their armaments, will be pretty much utterly useless. Any ships or submarines within striking distance of the EMPs will be immediately non-effective: dead.

"Missiles will stay in their silos unable to be launched because the entire United States is almost without any kind of power. Our chief ally has been taken out of the game in a moment.

"The assessment is an imminent threat of mass starvation, riots, the complete breakdown of American society and millions of deaths from the fallout alone. Obviously, this means we will not be an American priority in any way from now on.

"We are way down their list of things to do. Even if they want to help, they simply cannot do so. Their entire infrastructure has been so damaged it could take months if not years to bring them back up to speed."

Ben-Asher recoiled back into his chair and put his hands to his head. "And the American President?"

"No news, sir. We don't think they had time to get him safely onto Air Force One or even to a safe place on the ground before they were hit."

"Also on our home front, Mister Prime Minister, our missiles have been de-activated...shut down. We don't know how and we can't get them back online. Our entire defense system is dead. Sir, we are wide open to attack. The Russians, Iranians, Turks and their allies are pouring over the Golan Heights, moving fast with one intent: our total annihilation with nothing in their way.

"Latest Intel is the IDF is also having mechanical problems: barely any fighters can get in the air. We are on our own. They will not use Nukes on us because they want to take over the area."

"Are our military units active on the Golan?"

"They were, sir, but have suffered heavy casualties and have been forced to retreat.

"We believe a localized Russian EMP shut down all vehicles in the detonation area.

"Our forces are retreating on foot carrying the wounded and dying with them as best as they can with Russian and Iranian troops literally chasing them into Samaria with the Turkish army following close behind."

"Then," said Ben-Asher. "Israel ... is ... no more. The dream is over. Can this be the end of all our ancestors longed for? All our grandparents and parents worked and shed their blood for? My wife, my children... " He choked the words past his lips.

"My friends, we have no way to prevent the complete takeover of our people and our land by these forces." He could hardly look at the faces of his team. But his eyes connected with those of Rabbi Moshe Cohen.

"This may be our last few moments together. Rabbi will you please lead us in prayer one last time? Maybe, even at this late hour, Ha Shem will come to our aid."

Tears spilled down his face as he slid to his knees. Every person in the Situation Room hung their heads and knelt in prayer.

The Eighty-year-old Rabbi stood and quietly spoke through the sound of weeping around the room. "Oh, Almighty one. Ha Shem. God of our fathers Avraham, Yitzhak, and Yakov. We come before you as your ancient people, surrounded by our enemies: your enemies, oh mighty and eternal King of Israel. We have no help but you. No friend to call upon, but the God of our fathers. In this our hour of dire need with the threat of annihilation even at our very doors we beg you, beg you for mercy.

"We have strayed from your truths. We have forgotten..." The words ceased. All one could hear was the sound of weeping and the occasional choking plea from the Rabbi's lips. "Please, oh, Lord. Please help us."

Even as he spoke, there was a colossal shaking as if the entire area had been hit by a giant earthquake. Dust fell from the ceiling, creating a haze. Everyone was thrown to the ground, and the lights almost died. Some screamed in terror, believing this was the end. Then, all was quiet.

After a few moments, they picked themselves up and looked blankly at each other. Had the area above them been hit by a massive bomb of some kind? Was everyone above ground now dead?

They heard the sound of running and voices shouting outside the door. Was this it? Was the enemy, about to enter and finish off the entire Israeli leadership once and for all?

Ben-Asher took a deep breath and shouted: "Tsoomet Lev," the command to stand to attention.

Everybody stood and braced themselves for what was undoubtedly their fate: they were ready to make one last stand. Facing the door, they prepared to fight to the last man and woman and die for Israel.

Chapter 23

The door of the Israel Situation room burst open bringing the eyes of everyone present to full alert. An aide was waiving a newly printed intel in his hand.

"Mister Prime Minister, sir, we cannot understand this intel, but General Alon ordered me to rush this to you immediately.

"It seems to be totally opposite to all we have been receiving from the North."

Ben-Asher took the intel and wiped the tears from his eyes as he read the latest information from the battlefront.

"I, I don't understand this: How can it be? Is this a sick joke from our enemies?"

"Sir, it comes directly from the generals in the field."

Ben-Asher's hands trembled as he gazed at the news in disbelief.

"But we were on the brink of national destruction?"

He turned to the gathered political, intelligence, spiritual and military leaders who were looking at him. He held the sheet of paper above his head.

"Friends, the Russian, Turkish and Iranian forces are in full retreat. They are being bombarded from the sky with huge balls of fire. Also, a massive downpour has turned the area into a vast quagmire. Their tanks and land forces are unable to operate. Their planes have been swept from existence.

"They simply burst into flames and were seen to fall to earth. We have no idea how or why or by whom. Missiles were taken over by an unknown force and diverted into the sea."

Everyone stood in shock. "Are you certain of this?" asked the Prime Minister again in a whisper.

"Sir, we have reports from various sources, all repeating the same thing: our enemies have been destroyed without us barely able to lift a finger to stop them. They reached the hills in Samaria, but the entire invasion has come to a total halt.

"Their bodies are everywhere. Tanks and vehicles at a standstill. Some soldiers tried to run but were struck down by huge hailstones. Others died from the falling fire. Just a few survivors are struggling in sheer panic to get back to their lines."

"Was it the Americans who stopped them?"

"Highly doubtful, sir. They did manage to launch some missiles in our defense before they went down, but they failed to prevent the enemies advance. From what we understand almost the entire USA is on total shutdown. "

Ben-Asher looked around the room, searching for an answer.

"Then, who destroyed our enemies?"

Rabbi Cohen stood slowly to his feet, his tears running through his gray beard.

"Mister Prime Minister, Yitzhak. There is only one who could have saved Israel, this day. Our God has answered our prayers with fire and fury poured upon our enemies. He opened his well worn Tenach to the book of Yechezkel (Ezekiel) chapter thirty-eight, verse eighteen to twenty-three. "*On that day, when Gog comes against the land of Israel, says the Lord God, my wrath shall be aroused. For in my jealousy and in my blazing wrath I declare: On that day there shall be a great shaking in the land of Israel; the fish of the sea, and the birds of the air, and the animals of the field, and all creeping things that creep on the ground, and all human beings that are on the face of the earth, shall quake at my presence, and the mountains shall be thrown down, and the cliffs shall fall, and every wall shall tumble to the ground. I will summon the sword against Gog in all my mountains, says the Lord God; the swords of all will be against their comrades.*

With pestilence and bloodshed I will enter into judgement with him; and I will pour down torrential rains and hailstones, fire and sulphur, upon him and his troops and the many peoples that are with him. So I will display my greatness and my holiness and make myself known in the eyes of many nations. Then they shall know that I am the Lord."

The entire room stood in astonishment at the old Rabbi's words.

"My friends, do you not see? God has come down to rescue his people. He who watches Israel neither slumbers nor sleeps and he has destroyed our enemies once again as he did in days gone by."

Gently, he reached out trembling hands to those on his left and right and slowly, in a voice cracked with emotion, began to sing am Israel chai. The people of Israel live.

The entire group began to rotate gently around the conference table gathering speed as they did so. Then, in a moment, bursting into life, they threw their arms around each other and began dancing, singing, weeping, shouting.

As they danced faster and faster, they exploded with joy at the miracle that had just taken place. Twisting and leaping, crying in sheer relief, hugging each other, they encircled the room they had believed would be their sepulcher and danced as never before.

Although they could not adequately express the euphoria welling within them as they leaped around the room, one thing they knew for absolute certain: not only do the people of Israel live: the God of Israel also lives and had delivered his chosen nation from certain destruction.

Chapter 24

The destruction of the United States was apocalyptic. The detonations on the West coast vaporized millions of souls and buildings in a moment, with deadly nuclear fallout and the following winds of over a hundred mile an hour, destroying most of what structures remained.

The continuing seismic upheavals caused by the bombs resulted in the San Andreas Fault erupting with a ferocity never seen before.

Almost one-third of the Californian tectonic plate slid into the Pacific Ocean causing further millions of deaths. Even more, were brought about when earth responded with a new ten-point earthquake.

Fleeing people were lifted bodily by the force of the quakes and thrown over fifty feet into the air only to come crashing down onto the freeways packed with panicking drivers making a futile attempt to escape what was certain death.

In San Francisco, the Golden Gate Bridge, packed with traffic, was sent swaying to and fro as if it was paper caught in a gale force wind. Colossal mushroom clouds rose over the city and beyond. Gradually, almost majestically the bridge swayed over at an angle and then crashed with a roar of steam, foam and spray taking thousands with it to the bottom of the Bay.

Even so, some managed to survive and were seen frantically trying to swim to shore. Children and parents were seen desperately clinging to each other as the bridge, and the tide finally dragged them beneath the waves.

Planes attempting to take off from Los Angeles were thrown together by the forces of nature and the weapons of America's enemies, resulting in titanic explosions that ripped through the air throwing metal, glass and body parts to the four winds.

Following this calamity, long dormant magma beneath San Francisco erupted causing yet more death and destruction, making the nineteen hundred and eight quake look like a slight tremor. Roads were jammed with vehicles, but there was no escape.

Freeways were suddenly split open, and hundreds of vehicles slid into the widening chasm.

In a matter of moments, millions across the nation were being hurled into eternity.

Hollywood, the movie capital of the world and its surrounding area, vanished as the earth tipped and rocked like a ship in a storm and then altogether imploded with a roar accompanied by the screams of the doomed and dying. Rich and poor, famous and unknown fell together into the yawning, fiery abyss.

Across the nation, a series of strategically directed neutron bombs completely deactivated missiles still in their silos. Very few were able to launch before being made inoperative.

The death toll was not so enormous in these areas as the neutron bombs simply rendered all cars, planes, military vehicles of any kind useless.

On the East Coast, the news was much the same as was witnessed in the West of the country. The entire United States was a disaster zone that exceeded Biblical proportions.

New York resembled the city of Hiroshima at the end of the Second World War when the first Nuclear bomb was dropped on Japan.

Now, the mirror image appeared on the American Continent. People in the subways were vaporized, leaving only their shadows seared on the walls amongst the graffiti.

The Empire State building stood burnt out with smoke ascending from many of the windows. Chunks of masonry had been ripped away by the force of the nuclear blast, giving it the appearance of having been shelled.

Office workers there and in other high rise buildings were vaporized where they worked; the attack had come so suddenly.

People everywhere tried desperately to call loved ones, but all lines were dead.

The Hudson River had all but disappeared. Somehow the river had evaporated to the point of being fifty feet in width.

On either side, boats and ferries rested at awkward angles on the dried river bed.

Some showed signs of recent desperate efforts to escape. Bodies, packing cases and backpacks lay scattered around the decks and along the muddy shoreline.

Within weeks, violence, disease, starvation, and radiation led to painful lingering deaths. In some areas, cannibalism was not uncommon. Civil war erupted between factions up and down the continent, fighting for food and medical supplies.

Both were dwindling fast.

Aid was slow getting in from Europe, South America, and Canada. Some Arab nations offered to help, but many also saw it as Allah's punishment on the "Great Satan."

Many Christians in the surviving nations also

began to view America's demise as Heaven's punishment for her turning against God and causing much of the West to follow her lead.

Unlike past World Wars, the Third World War lasted a total of twenty-four hours.

Incredibly, much of Europe, Africa and the Middle and the Far East escaped anything akin to the fate of America, Russia, Turkey, and Iran.

All these nations were devastated, some more than others. But while the USA was destroyed by Russia and her allies, Russia and her co-conspirators were wiped out by what was at that moment believed to be an alien intervention.

The news was awash with stories of alien craft strafing Russian tanks and diverting missiles with mysterious rays as they swooped over the battlefront.

But it was all lies. While the secret leaders of the world had planned the war and the destruction of Israel they knew God had intervened ruined their plans and saved the Jewish nation. They refused to tell the truth to the people on the street and called in their spin doctors to spread lies. They purposely deceived the planet into believing beings from another dimension were their saviors.

But God had entered human history as predicted thousands of years before by the Hebrew prophets.

However, the demonic realm worked well in producing false images of UFOs sweeping across the Middle East to stop the global destruction before it was too late.

The world that had rejected the God of the Bible clung desperately to the great satanic lie.

Any talk of God having rescued Israel was viewed as the ravings of a lunatic.

This was a new world in search of a new leader, a new Messiah who would bring them back from the edge of global self-extermination.

And in the depths of Satan's kingdom, the plan was already in motion to give the world what it craved: the Antichrist.

Chapter 25

The little Christian group had witnessed the carnage from the safety of the safe house tucked deep within the Sussex countryside.

Hal had managed to SKYPE the office by sending a signal through a whole series of surviving channels across the planet ensuring it was virtually impossible to trace the source.

The inside news he received was stunning: America was little more than a Third World nation, though efforts were in progress to restore much of the infrastructure.

The Russian military and its allies had been destroyed by an unknown force believed to be from outside our planet.

The UK had barely managed to survive. Millions had died as a result of one nuclear detonation in the center of London. Most of the government was wiped out, and the resulting fallout had been catastrophic. However, most of Europe had come out of the war intact.

The reason became clear: Russia had wanted to take over Europe and the Middle East, so when the war erupted, it was over so quickly the Europeans barely had any time to gather their forces together with any planned defensive or offensive strategy.

An emergency meeting was planned in the hurriedly set up new United Nations center in the newly rebuilt city of Babylon, Iraq.

The extraordinary conference to be held at the headquarters of CERN in Switzerland had now been brought forward and was due to take place within the next week.

"You see," Hal said. "The planned meeting at CERN has not even been shaken by the recent war. I managed to hack into CERN system and found the meeting is due to take place next Monday. In fact, the war has driven the elite to immediate action, and we must be in Geneva within the next five days.

"An enormous clear up operation is underway in Israel, but America is devastated and so is Russia.

"Meanwhile, the elite are simply doing business as usual. They are in cahoots with these so-called alien saviors and cannot wait to bring forth the world's supposed new savior: Emmanuel Kohav."

"And maybe this meeting at CERN will do just that, do you think?" Asked Jack.

Hal smiled. "Think of what we saw on the flash drive. It's obvious, Jack. I have every suspicion what takes place at CERN will be an earth-shattering, history-making event and one at which you and Aaron must be present to witness, and hopefully, manage to survive and return safely to us so we can then expose the results to the world. Thank God flights to Europe are pretty much back to normal. I am amazed things in Europe have managed to get back on track so quickly.

Tomorrow we can drive to Lydd where my plane is and hop over to Geneva in readiness for the CERN event."

The following morning the drive to the airport took no more than forty-five minutes. The little group made their way to the hanger where Hal's G550 Gulfstream was waiting fully fuelled up and ready to fly the one hour, twenty-five minutes to Geneva. While the others busied themselves unloading the small amount of luggage they had hurriedly packed, Hal and Jack climbed aboard and began going through the flight plan.

"Better contact the tower," Hal flicked the switch connecting him to the flight controller.

They stowed the baggage away while Aaron drove the car to the parking bay.

"Hallo control, over."

"Is that you, Mister Montgomery? Over."

"Yes. Over."

"Could you come up here, please sir? I need a private word with you. Over"

"What's up? Over"

"Oh, it's just a security matter, sir. I need to go through it with you quickly. Over." He sounded nervous. Hall turned to Jack, who was busily checking the instruments.

"I don't like the sound of this, Jack. This hasn't happened before. It may be simply added security after the war, but I think you'd better be ready to high tail it out of here if I run into any trouble."

"How will I know what's going on up there in the control tower while I am down here on the tarmac?"

"If you don't see me in the next ten minutes get the heck out of here."

"Leave you here?" Jack defiantly placed his hands on his hips. "You are genuinely kidding me! No way. I'm not leaving you here. We said earlier we are in this together and now you're being the hero and saying we should leave you behind?"

"Jack, this is the most crucial mission any man has been on since the world began. I am not even sure we can change anything: prophecy is written in stone so it may be a lost cause anyway. But we can't sit by and let Kohav, the pope and their demon friends take over the planet without a fight. If you attend that meeting and leave there knowing for sure who he and pope Julius are we can at least try to spread what we know to be the truth.

"Even if we manage to spread the news of what you and Aaron witness at the meeting and what we have stored on the flash drive, it will at least wake some people to what they are up to, and it will be worth the effort. We have to do something," He laid his hand on Jack's arm. "Jack, you know I am right." Bridger looked down at his shoes heaved a sigh and shrugged. "Okay. I know, I know. You're the boss. But ten minutes, alright?"

Hal flicked the communication switch.

"Hallo control. On my way."

As he climbed out of the plane, the others looked at Hal in puzzlement.

"Hal, what's up?" asked Stacey. "Just checking some last minute paperwork in the control tower," he replied. She frowned.

"That's new."

"I guess it's because we filed the flight plan a little late. Be back in a minute," he kissed her on the cheek and strode toward the tower.

He entered the control tower building and climbed the stairs. Once at the top he knocked on the door and entered the control room. The moment he walked in the room the look of terror on the flight controller's face told him all he needed to know. That and his assistant's unconscious body sprawled on the floor.

"I'm sorry Mister Montgomery. He forced me to call you." The door closed suddenly behind Hal, and a voice said "Thanks, Mister Montgomery."

Hal swung round to face a fat, smiling Bald head, bulging eyes, and flabby white almost albino skin. It reminded Hal of a giant slug.

But this slug was holding a gun.

"Flash drive, now."

"What drive?" he bluffed.

"We don't have the time to get clever."

"No," replied Hal, becoming angry with himself for falling for the ruse to get him to the tower. "I can see getting smart would take quite an effort on your part."

Hal regretted his attempt at being funny as the fat one swung a muscle-bound arm and his fist smashed into Hal's abdomen sending him retching to the floor.

"The flash drive: where is it or do we ask your wife to come up for a chat?" He hauled Hal to his feet.

Gasping for breath, he looked down and saw

Stacey and the others lined up beside the plane, waiting for Hal's return.

The man yanked Hal back before they saw him and threw him into a chair. "Two minutes to think about it, then you and they are dead meat, understand?

"You've completely messed with the wrong people. Now we could kill you all, but we also need to be certain you haven't shared the information with anyone else," he looked at his wrist and grinned. "One minute fifteen seconds. Remember, I want the truth and no bluffing."

"Do you think we'd carry it with us?"

"Yeah. I think you'd carry it with you."

Suddenly the controller, a short, wiry man with a thin mustache and no chin, began to vomit. The villain with the gun was taken off guard for a split second as the door behind him opened.

He turned around just in time to see Aaron swing a crowbar at his gun hand. As the iron broke his wrist, the gun went off and flew out of his hand across the floor, the bullet narrowly missing Aaron's head and burying itself in the wall.

Hal was on his toes and grabbed the man by the neck from behind, trying to pull him back off balance. But the thug was a big brute and bent forward, lifting Hal off his feet. He then shot his elbow backward into Hal's rib cage, making Him release his hold and go sprawling on his back gasping for air again.

Aaron let fly with the crowbar into the man's legs. There was a crack of bone, and with a howl of pain, he crumpled to the floor. But he wasn't finished. He lashed out wildly as Goldberg leaped on top of him, his knees on each arm.

But the man was as strong as an ox, and he lifted Aaron sending him flying onto his back. As he did so, he swung his fist, catching Aaron under the chin, knocking him cold.

Hal staggered to his feet facing his enemy as the man lifted himself off the floor, dragging his broken leg after him. He made a swing at Hal.

A shot rang out.

A look of surprise crossed his face as a crimson stain slowly spread across his shirt. He glanced down at it, then at Hal, then at the controller who was shaking like a leaf and holding the gun. The slug coughed, made a gurgling sound and fell to the floor. His bulging eyes still open, staring into space. The controller threw up again.

Hal knelt down and bent over Goldberg, who was slowly coming to, holding his jaw.

"Aaron, are you okay?"

Aaron blinked and looked around.

"What happened?"

"I'll tell you as we move. Let's go."

"What about the body? Is that guy dead?" Aaron gazed down at the lifeless form soaking the carpet with his lifeblood.

Hal took hold of the controller's arm and gently shook it. "Hey, buddy. You okay?"

The man simply stared at the corpse and nodded, trying to make sense of what had just happened.

"Call the police. Tell them this man attempted to take over the control room, which he did. Tell them there was a struggle over his gun and you shot him in self-defense, which you did.

"Now, remember, struggle, gun, self-defense. Got it?"

The man nodded as his friend on the floor slowly came to and groaned.

Hal looked back at Aaron, "He'll be okay apart from a sore head.

Check the dead guy's pockets, Aaron."

Aaron knelt beside the body and with trembling hands proceeded to search it. He felt the man's trouser pockets They were empty, so were his jacket's outer pockets. When he put his hand into the inside pocket, he withdrew a wallet. Just a few notes and nothing else. Whoever was attempting to stop them, they were not going to leave calling cards.

After Hal watched Aaron go methodically through the dead man's scant belongings, he said, "The controller's testimony may hold the authorities off for a while. But it's a sure bet this guy was an employee of some high ranking demi-god in the shadow government.

"This thing goes higher than we can ever imagine. They will not want a fuss, so I guess once our friend here gives the police his story it will be swept under the rug. "

"One thing, Aaron," Hal said.

"I know," Goldberg replied.

They both said in unison, "How did they know we would be here?"

Hal grimaced. "It's pretty clear they have tabs on us. The people behind this certainly checked me out and found out about the plane. So they had a plant here and are probably watching seaports and major airports. I am surprised they only sent one man here, though. Thank God. Okay, let's get back to the others and get moving."

The plane landed in Geneva without incident. Hal and the others quickly disembarked and after getting through customs grabbed a cab and checked in at the Hotel Marianna perched on the shores of Lake Geneva.

For the next few days, they stayed around the Hotel and in their rooms going over what little plans they had.

On the evening of the CERN meeting, Hal gathered everyone in his and Tracey's room.

"Okay, so are we clear? Everyone stays here until Jack and Aaron get back from CERN headquarters. No one leaves the Hotel until they return and we all pack and leave for the airport together. The powers that be will be looking out for us as by now they realize we slipped through the trap they planned for us at the airfield.

"They may have tracked my plane and even suspect we have discovered the planned event and will be heading for CERN in the hope of infiltrating the meeting. But they can't be sure so they will be on full alert. Because of that, we must make a swift exit once Jack and Aaron return with the car Dinah hired. Are we all clear on today's events?" Everyone nodded.

"Okay. Aaron and Jack leave for CERN at seven tonight: that's in forty-five minutes time.

That should give them plenty of time to arrive, get into the building and mingle with the other guests."

"What do we do while we wait for Jack and Aaron to return?" Tracey asked.

"We pray," replied Lauren with a smile that hid the attack of nerves she was feeling.

"The girl learns fast," Jack laughed in an attempt to sound more confident of surviving the evening than he was.

"Before you both head out, let's pray now for God's protection on us all tonight, but especially on Jack and Aaron." Hal stood and bowed his head as everyone joined him, holding hands in a little circle.

When they had finished, Hal looked at his watch. "Okay, seven o'clock, boys. May the Lord be with you and protect you. Be careful. You are entering a place that tonight will be the abode of demons. If your identities are discovered, Kohav and the pope will not hesitate to have you both killed. Do you still want to do this?"

Jack and Aaron looked at each other and nodded. "We need to witness this event, so there will be no doubt in our minds when we share what we know about Kohav being the Antichrist," Aaron said with a slight nervous tremor in his voice. "Tonight I believe we will get the absolute proof."

Hal closed his eyes and nodded. "Okay. We will be in prayer until we hear from you. If we don't hear by one in the morning, I am afraid we'll have to leave without you."

Marsha burst into tears and flung her arms around Jack's neck. "I can't bear the thought."
Jack lifted her chin and tried to grin. "Hey, it will be okay. We will be back here before you know it. Just keep praying."

She nodded and ruffled his hair, "Okay. But you'd better not be lying to me, Jack Bridger or else." She tried to hide her tears and gave a weak smile as they rested their foreheads together, then kissed.

Aaron looked at Dinah. His mouth quivered as he wondered if this was the last time he would see the love of his life. He straightened up and hugged her. "Be back soon. Don't worry." He kissed her full on the lips, then turned and walked out the door with Jack. Neither dared look back.

Chapter 26

A light snow was falling as the Bombardier Global Express XRS private jet taxied to a standstill at Geneva airport's VIP area. The ground crew and airport security scurried around the exterior to ensure maximum privacy as the plane disgorged its passengers, warmly coated against the cold evening air.

Politely shepherding the dignitaries, they hurriedly transferred them to two waiting limousines, motors purring, on the tarmac.

The cars slowly pulled out onto 385 Route de Meyrin. Thirty minutes later they entered the private parking area beside the entrance to the massive CERN facility, the European organization for nuclear research, which straddles the French-Swiss border.

CERN's Director General, chief physicist Pierre Colbert stepped forward to greet his guests, warmly shaking their hands and bowing.

"Is all prepared?"

"Yes, your Holiness. All is ready. I am so honored to be permitted this great privilege to be a part of such a momentous event. The whole world has been awaiting this moment for thousands of years." Colbert beckoned his guests into the facilities warm interior.

Pope Julius and his entourage, including the Vatican's own Roman Catholic physicists, moved inside the building, passing the statue of Shiva the Hindu goddess of earth's destruction standing outside CERN's main entrance.

Once inside they were greeted by several other leading CERN dignitaries as well as politicians of every hue from around the planet, including leaders from all major world religions and of course the higher echelons of the global elite. All were out in force this evening.

Aaron Buchman, world Judaism's leading Rabbi, stepped forward arm in arm with Mohamed Fawzi, Islam's Grand Mufti of Jerusalem. Julius embraced both men, tears beginning to well up in his eyes.

"What a day, what a day," he said, his voice choked with emotion.

"Indeed my friend," Fawzi gripped the pope's hand in both of his. "As you say, what a day."

An official stepped forward. "Honored Ladies and Gentlemen, if you would please come this way."

Shaking hands with the other notaries and those accompanying Buchman and Fawzi, the group moved deeper into the facility.

Pope Julius turned to Colbert.

"You and your team have done an incredible service for mankind. One we can never repay."

"Believe me; it has been an amazing journey. One we could never have achieved had the world been truly aware of our attempts to break through the barrier into the next dimension," he rubbed his hand across his forehead and continued. "The few conspiracy theorists who latched onto our true intentions, we have for the best part, been able to portray as members of the lunatic fringe. As a result, we have been able to keep our discovery from the world.

"Sadly, those who came too close to revealing our work had to be removed permanently. But for the greater good. Even the frequent visits to CERN by Vatican scientists, we have been able to keep pretty well under the radar."

"In order to keep to the path we have taken, and for the betterment of mankind, it was necessary for intruders to be removed," Julius responded. "In the pursuit of mankind's growth, small-minded non-visionaries who refuse to see the greater picture have to suffer. A sad but necessary truth. May you be absolved," he made a swift sign of the cross above Colbert's forehead. "In the name of the Father, Son, and Holy Ghost. Amen."

"Thank you, your Holiness," Colbert bowed his head in gratitude.

The group continued walking.

Presently they entered the large area containing the Hadron Collider, the giant machine used for sending protons traveling at almost the speed of light in opposing directions around the vast 17-kilometer circumference of CERN until they collide producing a miniature reproduction of the big bang that supposedly created the universe.

To the world, this was the main area of research the physicists at CERN were involved in discovering.

But the truth was hidden far from the prying eyes of the uninitiated workers and scientists employed in the day to day research at the facility.

The group moved into a conference room and took their seats as the head of CERN stepped onto the podium at the front of the room. Doors were closed and locked as he gazed around the assembled dignitaries.

Jack and Aaron entered the building, keeping their heads down to avoid the security cameras. Once safely inside, they sat at the rear of the assembled guests. Jack turned to Aaron and said, "I hope no one can hear my heartbeat. It's thumping in my ears and chest so loud."

"Mine too," Aaron replied. "Let's pray we can sit this out and see what these devils have planned for this evening and get out as soon as it's over. I just hope everyone else is safe back at the Hotel."

"As long as they keep their low profile and act like simple tourists they should be fine," replied Jack.

The head of CERN began. "Good evening. It is with a sense of immense pride and satisfaction that I greet you on this historic occasion.

"This unique emergency meeting has been called for by the Vatican and the European Union following the tragic and devastating war between the USA and Russia and the attempted invasion of Israel by Russian, Iranian and Turkish troops accompanied by their allies. As you know this resulted in their destruction.

"Also, as most of you are aware, for the last few decades has CERN been acknowledged as the leading, if not the only, facility seeking to break into and solve the mystery of our beginnings from the event we call the big bang. In quantum physics and the search for other life forms in other dimensions, we have led the way.

"For those few of you who are not fully aware of our history, both public and secret, allow me to take a few moments to share our illustrious past with you as we, on this auspicious occasion, anticipate tonight's history-making, event.

"Besides being the mother and father of the modern internet, CERN's antecedents go back to the early part of the twentieth century and a man many believe to have been the embodiment of evil. Indeed Aleister Crowley did possess some traits that were far from acceptable to society. He identified himself as the wickedest man in the world. His so-called sexual magic, constant drug taking and supposed involvement in black magic rituals are ample food for internet bloggers of today.

"He even changed the spelling of his name so, according to ancient Gematria, the numerical sum of his name amounted to the number six hundred and sixty-six. The number attributed to the biblical embodiment of evil, the Antichrist.

"But behind the image religious bigots and others have painted of Crowley, what many do not know is the fact that he laid the path for what we have been quietly attempting to bring to fruition. One of his disciples was a man whose name may be familiar to many. Jack Parsons was a physicist who became one of the founders of the Jet Propulsion Laboratory in California.

"Parsons was one of the fathers of modern rocket science. Also, he became the leader of the American branch of Crowley's esoteric group the Ordo Templi Orientis. But I am running ahead of myself.

"In 1917 Crowley conducted an experiment: the Alamantra Working. In performing this ritual, he attempted to open a portal to another dimension. If he is to be believed, he succeeded, even bringing a living being named Lam through to our world. When Lam departed Crowley closed the portal.

"Now back to Crowley's disciple Jack Parsons. In 1946, Parsons and L. Ron Hubbard, founder of Scientology, decided to attempt a repeat of Crowley's ritual. They named their ritual the Babalon Working.

"Like Crowley before them, it involved a form of sexual magic which I shall not expand upon here. By all accounts, they succeeded in opening a portal. However, for some reason, they were unable to close it. It remained open.

"It is interesting to note that just a few months later the whole phenomenon of Unidentified Flying Objects hit the headlines. The first real encounter being on the West coast of America involving businessman Kenneth Arnold who coined the name Flying Saucers from the shape of the objects he saw and the way the discs skimmed along above the Mount Ranier mountain range akin to stones bouncing across a lake.

"What the world does not know is that we have continued these experiments, though not using such crude methodology as Crowley, Parsons, and Hubbard. We scientists, Physicists, and technicians who are specially chosen for the task have continued, behind the veil of finding the God Particle, reproducing in miniature the big bang.

"Of course, not every person working for CERN has been aware of our real purpose. We allowed them to believe our work evolved from the big bang to the discovery of other dimensions. But the search for contact with the other dimensions has always been our raison d'être. Many scientists have awakened to the fact this was the purpose of CERN all along, but they are few and far between, and most are on board with our plans.

"The truth of the matter is we have been in contact with the beings that pilot the UFOs for many years and tonight is the final culmination of our joint efforts.

"Different writers of UFO lore have discovered the so-called aliens are not from another planet but from another dimension. Authors, astronomers, and scientists such as Dr. Jaques Valee, the late Dr. J Allen Hynek of Project Blue Book, the American investigation into UFOs, and researcher and author John Keel came to understand the beings we are now in contact with are not extraterrestrial but extra-dimensional.

"They concluded the beings have a similarity to episodes of so-called demonic encounters. But that is where we disagree. We have found our contacts to be incredibly intelligent, spiritual beings.

"Your holiness is fully aware of those involved in the Vatican's scientific and astronomical endeavors who have met and interacted with these higher spiritual beings." Pope Julius pursed his lips and nodded.

Colbert spread his hands as he continued to address the global elite. "And of course, we are all aware of the superb work conducted by the Jesuit run Mount Graham Observatory in

Arizona in relation to observing our spiritual betters as they entered our dimension from their own and piloted their incredibly technically advanced craft across our skies.

"They observed us from afar and even in close encounters with various individuals. And their observations of humanities continued warlike nature so concerned them they brought forward the plan of the ages: to bring forth a leader not of this earth but of their own kind to save mankind from what would otherwise be our inevitable self-destruction in a global nuclear holocaust.

"The benign spirit that governs our dimension and the many thousands of others dimensions throughout creation could not allow this tragedy to befall us poor fallen children of Eve. Such is the love of the Divine universal spirit for us all, regardless of what faith path we may follow or even our total lack of faith in his existence. I fully believe it is he who has summoned us here this evening.

"Tonight we are on the verge of the greatest event since the Christ spirit last entered a human being. Honored guests, this very night as we stand at a pivotal point in our evolution, we invoke the spirit of the Universal Christ, that inhabited all the great leaders of the past including the Buddha, Jesus Christ and prophet Mohammed, peace be upon them.

"Through our research and indeed our contact with the elder brothers from the next dimension, and through our collaboration with leaders of almost every faith on earth we call upon that same Christ spirit to come and help us at this critical time in our history.

"The same Great Spirit entered Jesus Christ at his baptism and led prophet Mohammed centuries later, peace be upon him. He has deigned to come again to be our guide to truth. But the divine one requires a particular type of human vessel in which to reside. One who is prepared and ready to be endued with power from on high. Just as Jesus was filled with the Spirit at his baptism, so the chosen one will tonight be blessed as the Christ spirit enters him in the same way.

"Those of you who have visited CERN in the past have often asked the meaning and purpose of the ancient parchments we have on display. The languages are ancient Sanskrit and speak of the descent of the gods from the heavens to help and educate early mankind.

"The book of Enoch, the Bible and other ancient texts present the same history, although some do so in a biased way, depicting our brothers as fallen angels or even demonic beings. This, of course, is a total fabrication. These wonderful beings from beyond our dimension came with the very best of intentions.

"They are so much closer to the creator, their evolution over several eons being so much more advanced spiritually and technologically than our own," He bowed in reverence toward the pontiff and continued.

"Holy Father it is with deep gratitude we acknowledge your efforts over recent years to bring some kind of stability to this sad and some would say sin sick planet. Your efforts and those of your predecessors in the area of climate change.

"We remember your personal involvement in the Middle East peace process and your attempt to end the war in Syria. That war devastated so many lives and eventually brought us to the Third World War. With terror and tears, we witnessed the destruction of Russia and her allies as well as the United States once the conflict spilled over Israel's northern border. This madness woke the planet to the obvious but often ignored truth that we have the ability to eradicate our planet.

"At that moment when Russia, Iran, Turkey, and America were reduced to almost third world nations, by some miracle, a truce was called, and an unsteady peace followed. And now we are on the verge of a new dawn, a new world order if you will.

"As many of you are aware the source that ended the conflict we have just encountered was our elder brothers from the higher dimension.

"In order to prevent the complete destruction of all life on the planet in a nuclear exchange between the USA and Russia, our spiritual betters destroyed the forces invading Israel, but sadly not before the world's policeman, America herself was almost reduced to a wasteland.

"Now the mantle of global security has fallen to the expanding power of the European Union in partnership with the newly reformed United Nations now based in the rebuilt city of ancient Babylon.

"It seemed appropriate that as we embark on a new world order following the recent catastrophic conflict, the new United Nations should find its home where civilization had its beginning: ancient Babylonia, now modern-day Iraq. Also, with the aid of our brothers from beyond, we look for a world where all will live in peace under the governing spirit of God.

"My friends, if I may call you that, the whole world is crying for peace, stability, social justice, equality for all, food for the starving, a solution to the financial Armageddon we are now facing and the prayer for the dawning of a new world order of heaven on earth. Where all men are of equal value, nuclear war is abolished. We desire a world where every religion is united under the one, loving creator.

"We desperately need an end to religious diversity and an end to the scandalous threat of divine punishment for so-called sin. Such bigotry must be relegated to the archaic and spiritually ignorant past to which it belongs.

"To whom may we look for such a complete cure for man's ills? There is no one else to whom we may turn but to those who have recently protected us from our own destruction: those who came at our birth: who in ancient times taught us how to live together.

"These ancient gods from another dimension are returning to re-educate us in the use, and benefit, of natural remedies now long forgotten.

"Who else is more evolved technologically

and in closer union with our creator, but our ancestral masters from beyond this world?

"The human family must be guided into the new world order. Those who refuse to acknowledge the reality of our brothers' mission of peace will have to be re-educated in facilities already established and waiting for them now being made fully operational in the re-emerging United States under the control of the United Nations and the emerging Global Government.

"Sadly, those who continue to fight the new order will have to be eliminated for the good of the majority. We cannot continue this cycle of war and then peace followed by ever more destructive violence between nations. There must be total adherence to the new global order, or we shall simply embark on the same tragic journey with the same disastrous outcome we have just experienced.

"Our spiritual elders will not permit such elements to destroy the divine gift of life that has been granted to us. Sadly, such elements must be removed before they can cause us any further sorrow by spreading their cancer of hatred and bigotry.

"Tonight it is our hope, nay, our intention to introduce to the world a recognized human

Christ figure who would be far more acceptable to the human psyche. This is why we are gathered here tonight from almost every spiritual sphere on the planet.

"Many of you are the leaders of your respective faiths. It is to you your followers look for spiritual guidance. We have agreed over the past years, thanks again to Pope Julius, to come together as one spiritual body. It has taken a few years for many to see the truth of this universal spirituality where we are all children of the same creator whatever name we give him.

"The fundamentalists, of course, will always rebel. But given time and re-education, our prayer is that they too will wake to the reality that we are one world with one father and our brothers, our spiritual masters from beyond are endowed with a wisdom beyond our capacity to even dream of possessing.

"So how do we achieve this dream of presenting to the masses a leader whom they will all receive? A leader with the gifting and vision only possessed by those, not of this world? There has to be a physical impartation of true spirit: the Christ spirit that inhabits all holy men. Therefore, it became clear that the man, or being who will bring the global community together as one political and spiritual entity has to be one who is recognized by the majority of the planet. A man who is of this earth, yet not of this earth. Indeed, through the Hadron Collider after years of contact via the UFO phenomenon, we are, with their help, able to bring him here this very night through the Collider and present him to the world as the person the Theosophist Madam Blavatsky called the Universal Christ.

"This holy one, this holy being is willing to come to earth to help and guide us. And to allay the fears and superstitions of many spiritually ignorant he has deigned to inhabit the body of a man whom we all love, honor and admire.

"You know, of course, one of the Holy Father's title's in Latin is Vicarious Christi. In Greek, it translates as Anti Christos or Anti Christ. It means in the place of Christ. This one who will honor us this evening will be the true Anti-Christ. Not against Christ as many foolish Christians mistranslate the term, but one who operates in its truest meaning: in the place of Christ. He will be the final Vicarious Christi. The final Anti Christos who will lead the world into a new millennium of peace and union with God.

"The Holy Father, Pope Julius, has kindly condescended to assist the new Messiah as he enters our physical world from his spiritual dimension. For your kindness and humility, we are incalculably grateful."

Pope Julius stood and acknowledged Colbert's words as the room broke into spontaneous applause.

Julius took the stand, looking tanned, and youthful for all his sixty-five years. The Israeli Pontiff, was the first head of the church since the Apostle Peter became pope, though many dispute the idea the Apostle was ever a pope.

He cleared his throat. "Thirty years ago, a baby was born in the Middle East. He has become well known to many of us as he grew in favor with men and the creator. That man is here tonight: prepared to receive the impartation of the spirit of light, ready to embark on his divine mission to rescue the planet from destruction and place our feet once more on the path of enlightenment.

"This one man, the world's man of the hour, has willingly volunteered to take within himself the universal Christ spirit, the very being from the dimension we have been blessed to have been in secret contact with for decades. That same spiritual being inhabited the prophets of old including Jesus Christ." He nodded toward an aide at the rear of the room. The curtain parted, revealing a giant monitor on which all recognized the main Hadron Collider. The huge circular device towered above eight feet high four sided glass panels; each panel was five feet in width.

Julius continued "Ladies and Gentlemen, at this point in our evening, it is my greatest joy to invite the President of the European Union, Emmanuel Kohav to take his place before the Collider."

Emmanuel Kohav, dressed in a flowing, shining white thobe, also known as a kaftan, stepped from behind a curtain into the spotlight amidst gasps from the gathered company, many of whom had expected none of this when they were invited to attend.

The leaders and dignitaries rose from their seats in awe and excitement and broke out into spontaneous cheering and applauding as they anticipated what was about to take place.

Before their spiritually blinded eyes, they were about to witness an alien entity from another dimension entering and inhabiting the body of this willing volunteer.

Unknown to most delegates, Emmanuel Kohav would become the Antichrist: the physical embodiment of pure evil. The onlookers foolishly believed it was for the good of the planet. Also, they told themselves this act of human rebellion against God would herald a giant leap in mankind's spiritual and physical evolution as humanity became united with their spiritual masters from another dimension.

Jack and Aaron sat riveted to the spot in almost total disbelief.

"Oh, my dear Lord Yeshua," Aaron whispered.

"These fools are blind participants welcoming the beast of the book of Revelation: the beast from the bottomless pit. CERN has opened the pit. Or rather an angel has allowed this to happen by opening it for them in their evil pursuit of knowledge.

"Kohav is willingly prostituting and damning himself to become the evilest man in history: the Antichrist. That thing that is about to enter and guide him will make him the embodiment of pure evil. He is already the son of Satan, and this is his baptism." He shuddered.

Jack's face drained of color. "Are you saying...?"

"You know what I am saying, my brother. We saw this on the flash drive, and now it is in front of us. We are looking at the Antichrist and the False Prophet straight out of the book of Revelation. The beast from the bottomless pit has a name in Hebrew, it is Abaddon, in Greek Apollyon, which means the destroyer." He gripped Jack's bicep, "Hal was correct when he warned us that beast is about to enter our dimension, our world and inhabit the body of Emmanuel Kohav.

"The Antichrist, Emmanuel Kohav, is about to be unleashed upon the world along with Pope Julius as the False Prophet and there is not a thing we can do to stop it."

Chapter 27

Emmanuel Kohav stepped forward to the applause of the invited audience of the elite from around the world. He hugged Pope Julius, and the two held their joined hands aloft to the cheers of the adoring crowd.

After acknowledging the greetings, he signaled for the President of Israel and President Karahan of Turkey to step forward alongside Islam's Grand Mufti of Turkey and the Grand Mufti of Jerusalem in a show of peace and reconciliation.

Accompanying Israel's President were the members of the Sanhedrin, Judaism's leading religious scholars and the President of the Palestinian Authority Mohammed Darwaza.

As the cheers and applause subsided, Pope Julius stepped to the microphone. "Dear friends. What a blessed evening we are having are we not? Here beside me, you see a united front for peace in the Middle East. This again is due to the continued efforts of President Kohav. So in line with this and before we witness the coming of the Universal Christ, it is my blessed task to reveal some news to you that was purposely withheld until this evening's gathering."

He continued, "The terrible events, the horrors out of which we have only recently emerged, has made this meeting all the more urgent and needful to bring our world together in the bonds of peace and security.

"Friends, I have received this communiqué from the head of the United Nations, Doctor Emile Silva with permission to release it worldwide. In a private meeting which many of you attended, the United Nations has voted overwhelmingly to invite the President of the European Union, Emmanuel Kohav, to become the first President of Global Unity. In other words, Emmanuel Kohav is now President of Planet Earth."

The auditorium burst into loud cheers of acclamation as Kohav stepped forward to receive their adoration.

After several minutes of applause which the pope could barely bring to order, with Kohav standing beside him, Pope Julius continued,

"Of course you must understand the ultimate event about to take place this evening can only be released to the world when we feel it is ready to be received. But we can tell you of another wonderful undertaking information about which will be released immediately.

"As I said a moment ago, our dearly beloved brother, President Kohav has been working tirelessly behind the scenes with me to achieve unity between the Palestinians and Israelis. Between Islam, Judaism, and Christianity. These meetings and frank discussions have yielded unexpected and wonderful results. May we see the agreed design, please?"

The screen behind Julius lit up with an animated graphic of the Temple Mount. It was the same graphic Hal, and the group had seen on Aaron's computer screen.

As the graphic flew over the Mount, it settled facing the Dome of the Rock. Then gradually stone by stone a graphic of the Jewish Temple rose to stand beside the Dome on its northern side. The gathered delegates let out a roar of approval as everyone on the platform stepped forward in a line, with clasped hands raised above their heads.

Pope Julius and President Kohav stood in the center of the line and then stepped forward together to the cheers and applause of everyone present.

Julius held his hands aloft and spoke.

"Friends, what you see is the culmination of years of discussion between Israel, the Palestinian Authority, the Vatican, our alien brothers as well as our Turkish friends and the leaders of Islam also the kind interaction we had with the Jordanian authorities who oversee the Temple Mount some of whom are here with us tonight.

"After many centuries of hatred and mistrust, at last, we are agreed on this message to the world: Jews and Christians and Muslims can now worship together in peace and unity here in the Temple for all mankind. The instruments have been prepared over many decades of hard work by skilled artisans who have produced the very items used in the ancient Temple of Jerusalem. Now, it will not only be a Temple for Jewish people in which to worship and sacrifice, but it will truly be a Temple for all mankind to worship their God whatever faith they choose to follow."

The pope's voice rose with excitement. "The building will begin in the next two months and is expected to be completed in time for the Jewish Passover, when, for the first time in two thousand years, the priests of the Temple will sacrifice the Passover lambs in the presence of myself and President Kohav.

"All are welcome to attend and be a part of this new beginning once the Temple is built."

More thunderous cheers and applause issued

forth as the pope and Kohav acknowledged the crowd's adulation. Pope Julius smiled, "Yes, all will be welcome to come and worship in the Temple of Humanity. And now, dear ones, we move on to the main reason for our gathering tonight. The arrival of the Christ spirit. My dear friend, President of the European Union and President of the world, President Kohav, if you please."

After acknowledging the loud greetings without saying a word, Kohav was ushered through a side door by his aides and CERN technicians.

The pope took his seat as the head of CERN raised his hand and signaled toward the back of the auditorium. The lights dimmed, and the screen showing the Hadron Collider suddenly changed to reveal a large room with a huge upright glass cylinder. To some of those watching it looked similar to a huge shower cubicle, but for the fact, the top was encased in wires and attachments that they were fed directly through a series of multiple connectors to the Collider.

The director spoke. "I must emphasize that what you are about to witness is beyond top secret. I repeat, it is beyond top secret. No one outside this facility is to be told a word of what you are witness to this evening until the global authorities agree to release the information.

"President Kohav has volunteered to be the willing human vehicle for peace by welcoming the spirit that inhabited Jesus, Buddha, Mohammed and all the great spiritual leaders of the past to come through the Collider from his dimension into ours. In a gracious act of love, he will enter and take up residence in President Kohav's body for the furtherance of universal enlightenment of the human race as he embarks on his role as leader of the world."

Presently, Kohav appeared on the screen and was led to the cubicle. Once inside, and seated the door slid shut.

The whole auditorium was in rapt attention, their eyes glued to the screen. No one moved or uttered a sound as all eyes were focused on the cylinder.

Presently the sound of the Collider could be heard. Almost imperceptibly the cylinder began to take on a greenish hue. Kohav suddenly became rigid, upright, his eyes tightly closed. Then, to everyone's astonishment, a portal opened above his head.

As it did, a giant gray, reptilian face appeared and began to descend. Large, black soulless eyes stared from deep sockets. The almost nonexistent lips curled into a smile as the being merged into the face of Emmanuel Kohav.

Then in a moment, it was gone. Emmanuel Kohav looked the same as when he entered the cylinder. His eyes remained closed as the Collider gently reduced its revolutions.

Eventually, the whole place became quiet. Nobody moved. No one appeared to know quite what to do next.

The assistants moved to the cylinder door as it slid open. Kohav stood upright and stepped out. His eyes were now open.

But all color had vanished from them. They were completely black. Slowly the color returned to normal.

The baptism of the Antichrist was complete. In a demonic parody of the baptism of Jesus when the Holy Spirit entered him, the destroyer, Abaddon, the ultimate spirit of all that was anti-good and anti-God: the very personification of undiluted evil had risen from the bottomless pit and taken up residence in the willing body of Emmanuel Kohav.

Jack and Aaron watched the demonic proceedings in stunned, horrified silence.

They looked around at the crowd that had now risen to their feet in euphoric cheering and applause.

How could they all be so blind? Did they not know this was the possession of a human being by something beyond our realm? Yes, they did, and they didn't care.

They believed it was going to be the panacea for all the troubles of the world. With a new Messiah, a new world leader and new prophet all would be better than ever before in the world's history.

They had a Christ figure that would not be ridiculed or crucified, but instead would be adored and welcomed by the inhabitants of the earth.

In the pope, they also had a leader of a new global spirituality: one who would ultimately demand the worship of Emmanuel Kohav: the son of Satan.

Those who would not receive him would pay the ultimate price for what would be considered blasphemy.

After all, it would be reasoned, only wicked and blind fools would reject the planet's ultimate savior: a man entirely taken over by the spirit of the divine.

But they were wrong.

Jack and Aaron were the only ones in the room who knew the truth: Emmanuel Kohav was the Antichrist, Pope Julius was the False

Prophet. These were the men who would not bring everlasting peace, but the final judgment and fury of a holy God upon themselves and the rebellious inhabitants of the planet.

"I need to get out of here. I think we've seen enough." Jack motioned to make for the door while everyone was involved in celebrating. Aaron pulled out the two cards he had used to gain their entry that evening.

As he stood, there was a shout from the platform. The room immediately fell silent.

The pope was gazing around the auditorium. For one horrifying moment, Aaron felt it was as if Julius was looking directly at him and Jack but his eyes swept past them. His eyes were narrowed in anger, and he pointed. "Please stand where you are. I have just been informed that upon inspection of the number of admission cards, there are two that appear to be false. It is essential that we find and detain these two people. We fear they have infiltrated this meeting with malicious intentions.

"It is possible they have come to spread lies about this evening and cause hatred and division. They must be prevented from leaving. They must not leave the facility. Call security at once."

Security guards entered the hall, blocking the

doorway. Jack and Aaron were caught in the crowd streaming for the one exit where the guards at the door were taking their time carefully screening everyone.

A spirit of anger arose among the people.

"Find them. Don't let them escape."

Jack looked around for another exit. There was no other way out.

"We're stuck."

"Oh, Lord Jesus. Help us, please."

Aaron felt a hand rest on his shoulder from behind. He turned to see a young man in a dark suit smiling at him. He stood a little over six feet tall with jet black hair and olive complexion.

"Come with me and keep quiet." Dark brown eyes motioned them to follow.

"Who are you?" Jack stared at him.

"A friend. I have been sent here to help you."

Aaron could feel his pulse quickening as the young stranger moved closer to the guards, thinking any moment they would be identified as the interlopers.

As the three arrived at the door, the young man looked directly into the first security guard's face. The guard froze and seemed to be in a trance. He just stared into space.

"With me, now." The young man ordered.

The moment they had passed the security guard, he snapped awake and continued checking the guests following behind as if nothing had happened.

They walked past the line of armed security officers manning each side of the exit hallway, all of them standing and looking blankly ahead until they had passed by.

As the three men approached the main facility doors, they unlocked of their own accord and swung open, allowing them to pass through unmolested into the car parking area.

They strode across the car park and got into to the car, with the stranger taking the back seat. Aaron drove toward the barrier which lifted as if raised by an unseen hand.

Once safely on the highway, Jack turned to the man to ask again who he was. He wasn't there. He had vanished into thin air.

They were alone. He shouted, "The young guy...he's not there."

They pulled over to the side of the road and looked at each other in bewilderment.

"But he got in the back. I saw him."

"So did I, but he's gone."

"Aaron, I am up for believing anything these days. You don't suppose that was an angel?" Jack asked.

Aaron, who was as shocked and thrilled as Bridger, scratched his head. "I don't know, but...I guess so. That is the only explanation I have. Think about it. The guy came from nowhere, picked us out of the crowd trying to leave the building, got us past security, even got into the car, saw us through the barrier and then vanished." He slapped his hands on the steering wheel in sheer joy and shouted at the top of his voice.

"Hallelujah! God is with us, Jack. God is with us. He sent his angel to get us out of that place just like he did to the Apostle Peter when he was in prison. Did you see how the doors and the barrier just opened on their own? If he hadn't helped us get out of that situation who knows what those people's bosses would have done if they had found out who we are. They may have forced us to tell where the others are hiding. They may even have killed us. Instead, right now they will probably be having a massive argument with their security team and wondering how we slipped past them."

Jack laughed out loud with relief. "Aaron, do all Christians have this kind of thing happen?"

Aaron's shook his head. "Not often, Jack. But it has been known. I think we should pray."

They bowed their heads, and Aaron spoke.

"Abba, father. Thank you. Thank you so much. You sent your angel to rescue us. How marvelous are your ways oh, God. How we thank you for this incredible deliverance."

They drove away reveling in God's supernatural rescue mission. Aaron broke the silence. "Okay, so let's get back to the Hotel, tell the others what happened and pack."

"I know Hal said we must leave at once but where to? Where are we going?"

"Jack, my friend, we are going to Israel, the one place to which all these events are pointing.

We are going to Jerusalem. Prophecy centers on the Antichrist, Jerusalem and the Temple in the end times so it figures if the spirit of Antichrist has now taken over the person of Emmanuel Kohav, he and the False Prophet, Pope Julius will soon be making some historic moves involving the Middle East, Israel, Jerusalem and the plans we heard tonight about the rebuilding of the Temple. We need to be in the center of the wheel of prophecy. That center is Jerusalem.

"Tonight, Jack, we have been permitted by God to see something about which our Christian forebears could only speculate. As we watched Emmanuel Kohav and Pope Julius this evening, we were among the first people in history to look upon the Antichrist and the False Prophet.

"The days are short, my friend, Jesus is coming back soon, and we are now in possession of vital information that needs to be shared urgently with all who will listen: the Antichrist is among us. Are you in?"

Jack Bridger lowered his head in thought then lifted it and grinned. "Aaron, after all God has done for me recently and now the information he has allowed me to see revealed, to be joined with you and the others, the one place I don't want to be right now is *out*. All my life I have been outside the family of God and outside the knowledge of these, what do you call them, Last Days? Aaron, I'm in! Come what may, I am in this with you guys and for the people who we must warn. But most of all, I am totally in this for Jesus. But before he comes, let's get the word out while we are able. Jerusalem it is...let's go!"

TO BE CONTINUED

Made in the USA
Columbia, SC
26 December 2018